Constable Beats the Bounds

Nicholas Rhea is the pen-name of Peter N. Walker, formerly an inspector with the North Yorkshire Police and now the creator of the Constable series, which inspired the hugely successful TV series Heartbeat, and author of many very successful topographical books about Yorkshire and the Lake District. He lives in North Yorkshire. Visit the official Nicholas Rhea website at www.nicholasrhea.co.uk

By the same author

The Constable Series

Constable on the Hill
Constable on the Prowl
Constable Around the Village
Constable Across the Moors
Constable in the Dale
Constable by the Sea
Constable Along the Lane
Constable Through the Meadow
Constable in Disguise
Constable Among the Heather
Constable by the Stream
Constable Around the Green
Constable Beneath the Trees
Constable in Control
Constable in the Shrubbery
Constable Versus Greengrass
Constable About the Parish
Constable at the Gate
Constable at the Dam
Constable Over the Stile
Constable Under the Gooseberry Bush
Constable in the Farmyard
Constable Around the Houses
Constable Along the Highway
Constable Over the Bridge
Constable Goes to Market
Constable Along the River-bank
Constable in the Wilderness
Constable Around the Park
Constable Along the Trail
Constable in the Country
Constable on the Coast
Constable on View

CONSTABLE AT THE DOUBLE
Comprising
Constable Around the Village
Constable Across the Moors

HEARTBEAT OMNIBUS
Comprising
Constable on the Hill
Constable on the Prowl
Constable in the Dale

HEARTBEAT OMNIBUS VOLUME II
Comprising
Constable Along the Lane
Constable Through the Meadow

NICHOLAS RHEA

Constable Beats the Bounds

ROBERT HALE · LONDON

© Nicholas Rhea 2009
First published in Great Britain 2009
Paperback edition 2010

ISBN 978 0 7090 9116 5

Robert Hale Limited
Clerkenwell House
Clerkenwell Green
London EC1R 0HT

www.halebooks.com

2 4 6 8 10 9 7 5 3 1

Typeset by Derek Doyle and Associates, Shaw Heath
Printed in the by the MPG Books Group, Bodmin and King's Lynn

Chapter 1

Beating the Bounds

'Rhea!' barked the instantly recognizable voice of Sergeant Blaketon one morning soon after I assumed my role as constable of Aidensfield. He rang as I was preparing for my day's duty in the splendid countryside around the village. Fortunately I was in my own office adjoining the police house, fully uniformed and on the point of departing upon a quarterly check of some livestock registers at Crampton and Elsinby. 'Are you perchance heading for Ashfordly today?'

To be honest, I had no intention of visiting Ashfordly Police Station for I had no reports to submit for his scrutiny and signature and besides, I wanted to get the livestock registers checked. I'd just enjoyed two weekly rest days so my desk was clear and all my report writing was up to date. However, I felt I'd better give him the answer he clearly expected.

'Yes, Sergeant, I need to check my in-tray.'

'Yes, you do. That's why I'm ringing, there's something in your tray that needs your immediate and undivided attention.'

'Right, well, thanks for telling me.'

'See me when you get here, and don't wait too long. I'm a busy man, as you know. Being the section sergeant means a hectic and responsible life with lots of duties to perform so I can't hang around waiting all day for you to turn up.'

'So what's so urgent and important for me?'

But he had already replaced his receiver and I did not get an answer. I was left wondering what on earth he wanted me to do now. Even after several years as the constable of Aidensfield I still remembered that particular morning. As I said, it was very early during my tour of duty in Aidensfield and it introduced me to aspects of life I'd never before encountered. It also gave me a better understanding of country life in the village to which I had been posted. In addition, of course, it meant I was privileged to gain a deeper appreciation of the people who worked and lived there. A short while later therefore, I arrived at Ashfordly Police Station and hurried into the duty office, but even before I could get my coat or motor-bike helmet off or even bid 'Good morning' to PC Alf Ventress, a strong voice called from the sergeant's office, 'Is that you, Rhea?'

'Yes, Sergeant.'

'About time too. Where have you been? I've been sat here twiddling my thumbs and waiting for hours. . . .'

'I came straight away, Sergeant, I've not been stopped on

the way to deal with anything and I've not been anywhere else. I got here as soon as I could.'

'You've not broken any speed limits getting here, that's pretty obvious. So now you've decided to grace us with your presence, come into my office and listen to what I'm going to tell you.'

And as I made for Sergeant Blaketon's office, Alf Ventress, behind the typewriter on his desk, merely shrugged his shoulders and smiled at me in sympathy as if to say, 'He's not in a very good mood today.'

As I walked in, Sergeant Blaketon was sitting at his desk with a mug of coffee at his side, but he neither invited me to have one, nor even to sit down. There was a chair beside his desk for use by important visitors like the superintendent or perhaps a local councillor. But not for me.

'Anything to report, Rhea?'

'All correct, Sergeant,' I trotted out the traditional response.

'Have you got that file from your in-tray?'

'File?'

'Yes, the one I put there not an hour ago, the one I rang you about.'

'You called me straight into your office as I arrived, Sergeant—'

'Don't answer back and don't just stand there. Go and get it then bring it in here. You need to study it with great care.'

I could see he was in one of his characteristic moods; clearly something had annoyed or upset him – probably his wife – and so I meekly obeyed and recovered the file. Alf produced another of his knowing smiles, but I couldn't pass comment because Blaketon would hear every word we said. I walked back into his office clutching the very heavy buff-coloured file. It was probably more than three inches thick with hundreds of documents all secured with a length of string, and then I saw the title on the front. It said, Beating the Bounds.

When I reached his desk, he said, 'Have you read it?'

'Read it, Sergeant? All this? Not yet. I . . . er, well, I've only just picked it up.'

'There are no excuses for slackness, Rhea. Right, you will have to take it away and read it carefully, then submit a report to outline your proposals.'

'Proposals?'

'Yes, that's what I said. Proposals. I need to study your proposals before we take any further action. That's if we need to get involved.'

'We?'

'Yes, we. Ashfordly Police, and when I say that I include references to assistance from all our rural officers. It's a big job, Rhea, one that will put our local officers in the spotlight so we need to get things right. That is why you have been specially selected to act as team leader in this exercise.'

'Oh, right, Sergeant. I'll read it immediately.' I had no idea what he was talking about, but knew better than to enter a discussion with him. As he had implied, everything I needed to know would be in the file.

'The sooner the better,' he said, and I thought I detected

more than a hint of a smile or a twinkling of his eye. I gained the impression he was enjoying my obvious discomfort. 'Look,' he said, 'I'd better explain. Two weeks this coming Thursday it will be Ascension Day and that's when the Parish of Aidensfield beats the bounds.'

'Beats the bounds?' I had heard that phrase used on occasions but wasn't sure what it entailed.

'The parish boundaries, Rhea. It happens every three years when the entire parish walks around the boundaries, taking a schoolful of children with them to beat them, and that makes them remember where the boundaries are. That's how people of bygone times learned where their village boundaries were. It was something they never forgot.'

'You mean they beat the children?'

'No, not any more. They beat the boundaries, or rather the children do. They thrash the boundaries with long pieces of hazel. They love doing that bit.'

'Oh,' I said with some relief whilst not sure what was actually going to happen.

He seemed to enjoy airing his knowledge as he continued, 'They used to beat the children at certain points around the boundary so they would never forget their position, but that was in the middle ages, we're much more civilized now. So you'll need enough pieces of hazel for all the kids and probably some spares in the event of breakages or losses.'

That's when I began to air my doubts with more than a little concern. 'But if this is a parish affair, Sergeant, why are we involved? I'd have thought members of the parish along with their councillors and other officials could walk around the boundaries and find enough hazel sticks to thrash them without the police being involved.'

'We need to know everything that goes on in our patch, Rhea.'

'I understand that, but I must say this sort of thing is hardly a police matter, Sergeant.'

'A police presence is needed to prevent disturbances, to keep order, to maintain the peace and prevent disputes about the actual positioning of the parish boundaries. We don't want neighbouring parishes claiming we have nicked a parcel of their land, do we? And we don't want them nicking bits of our parish either. Such things can lead to punch-ups or even outbreaks of civil war or worse. Just remember how World War II started, Rhea.'

'Oh,' I said, thinking it couldn't be that serious.

'And there is another point you need to be aware of, Rhea. For centuries, it has been the custom in Aidensfield for the constable to lead the perambulation of the boundaries. In former times, it was the constable who beat the kids when they misbehaved so the powers-that-be thought he should be just the fellow to beat them during the boundary perambulation. You don't have that honour now, of course, we don't beat children any more no matter how badly they behave, but you are still a key figure in the custom. It's your job to make sure the kids thrash the boundary markers so they remember where they are.'

'I don't know where they are, Sergeant. I know my own beat boundaries, but not the parish.'

'Then you'll have to learn fairly smartly, won't you? You need to know where you are going because you'll be leading the others. We don't want everyone getting lost, or trespassing onto neighbouring parish properties, or wandering into private estates and gardens during the perambulation. They'll think we're trying to pinch some of their land. We don't want trouble, Rhea. We have to make sure there's no trouble. The role of constable is to keep the peace and prevent crime. Got it?'

'Well, yes, but it will help to know exactly what my duties will be.'

'Which is why you've got that file to study, and why we need to know your proposals. As soon as possible, or even sooner.'

'Is there any record of the previous constable doing this? Or a succession of previous constables?'

'Everything will be in that file, Rhea, and you can expect the local newspaper to turn up too. Aidensfield's ceremony of Beating of the Bounds always makes a good piece of news, especially when someone gets lost, or a fight develops, or a dog attacks some sheep ... or whatever. You'd be amazed what can go wrong.'

'Thank you for that!'

'Well, Rhea, I expect you will make such a thorough job of finalizing the plans that nothing will go wrong. So it's over to you now. Find a quiet corner somewhere and study that file, then let me know what you intend to do. And, remember, your colleagues from Ashfordly Section are always available to give a hand if you need them.'

'Am I likely to need their help?' I asked innocently.

'Well, you will be fully committed on the day, leading the procession around the boundaries. You won't have time to deal with everything that happens when a crowd of a couple of hundred or more people and children, some with dogs or even horses, is on the move. You might need a constable on traffic duty on the main road to ensure the perambulating people get across safely – and don't forget the boundary runs right through the middle of the Sheep Breeders' Arms up on the moors, one half is in Aidensfield parish and the other is in Gelderslack.'

'That's not on my beat, Sergeant. The pub I mean.'

'No it's not, but part of it is within Aidensfield parish. Some of the perambulators like to stop there to refresh themselves and fights have been known to develop following allegations of trespassing into private land or inside the neighbouring parish boundaries. The parishioners of Gelderslack are a funny lot, Rhea, quite territorial in some ways. More of a clan than a parish.'

Because it was not on my beat, I had never had the need to check the Sheep Breeders' Arms so I was rather puzzled to find it was actually straddling Aidensfield parish boundary. Or to be precise, part of it was on the boundary. 'So why is the Sheep Breeders' Arms not on Aidensfield beat, Sergeant, if part is within our parish boundary?'

'It was extended some time during the 1800s and the new bit was in Aidensfield parish. They didn't have trouble with planning consent in those days. It meant the bar area never was within Aidensfield parish and in fact it is still not – it's within Gelderslack's boundaries. So you might gain a better understanding of the situation if some of our boundary beaters go into that bar during the perambulation. It could lead to a breach of the peace, if not the outbreak of World War III. If they go in at any other time, there is no problem, it's just when we are establishing the boundaries that trouble is likely to arise.'

'So will the Gelderslackians know when we are beating our boundaries?'

'You can bet on that, Rhea! Ascension Day is marked in their diaries and they will be watching all our movements that day, watching in case we try to nick a piece of their parish. They'll turn up at the pub in force, believe me, they're very proud of their own boundaries.'

'So if that pub straddles two parishes, is there anything else that sits astride our boundaries?'

'Funny you should mention that, Rhea. The boundary runs down the middle of Gelderslack Beck for about a mile.'

'I can't see folks getting fussy over a boundary that runs down the middle of a beck, Sergeant.'

'Well, I hope you're right, Rhea. But it does mean you have to wade along the bed of that beck, so you'll need to take fishing waders. It's quite deep in places but it's vital that every inch of the boundary is strictly perambulated.'

'Can't we just rely on maps, Sergeant? It seems a much simpler way of deciding things.'

'No we cannot rely on maps, Rhea. Maps have been known to get things wrong, probably quite deliberately at times, so the only way for us to establish our boundaries, beyond dispute, is to perambulate around them once every three years. That eliminates all doubt. And that is your task on this auspicious occasion. So off you go and make sure you look at every aspect of this most important of Aidensfield's civic duties.'

'Yes, Sergeant.'

'You must approach this task with pride and responsibility, Rhea. It means you will become part of history. Your part in the affair will be included in that file you've got.'

'Yes, of course, Sergeant.'

Studying the file was one example of how I could work at home for a while. If there was one phrase which caused senior police officers to think some kind of dodge was being practised, it was 'I'm working at home'. If I studied this file at home, therefore, albeit within the confines of my official office, I knew I would be treated with some suspicion by my colleagues and supervisory officers, even Blaketon who'd given me the task. In their view, I'd be far wiser to sit on my motor bike to read it among the rain and wind, and if I used an office in a police station like Ashfordly or Eltering, there'd be accusations of skiving. The supervisory officers of the police force were a highly suspicious bunch of individuals, probably because they'd discovered all manner of skives when they themselves were mere constables. However, in my mind that day, constabulary duties had to be done for the sake of local history and so I decided to go home and study the papers in the comfort of my own office. One advantage was that I would be available to any members of the public who might telephone or call for my attention; they liked their bobby to be available when needed. My decision made, I would telephone my Divisional Headquarters to explain where I was and what I was doing. That would stop them trying to contact me via the radio on my motor bike.

Mary was very surprised to see me return to the house and thought something was drastically wrong, but when I explained the situation she said it would be nice having me at home for the day or even just a few hours. Perhaps I could look after the children while she popped out to the shops? I tried to explain that I might be called out to some emergency such as a traffic accident, but she viewed my unexpected presence as a bonus not to be missed. And off she went to the shops.

After ringing DHQ with my plans, I settled down to read the bulky file which, I found, covered a period of more than fifty years — fifty-one to be precise. That was seventeen perambulations. In all cases, the village constable had led the Aidensfield perambulation and beating of the boundaries on Ascension Day every three years. The file dated back to 1913 and I wondered where the previous files were kept — probably in the loft at Ashfordly Police Station. There must be a wealth of important historical records up there, I decided.

Fortunately the children seemed settled and were playing happily in the garden when the superintendent rang in person from Divisional HQ.

'Rhea, what's all this about you working at home? Rural constables do not work AT home, Rhea, they work FROM home. You need to be on patrol, Rhea, out and about, showing the uniform and preventing crime. Not sitting at home waiting for things to happen.'

'I'm studying a file, sir, given to me by Sergeant Blaketon. He said it was very important and told me to find a quiet place to read it in depth. There's nowhere suitable at Ashfordly Police Station except the cells so I'm doing it at home. I'm available here for whoever needs me, police and public alike.'

'You could read it in your own time, Rhea.'

'It's an official file, sir, to be studied on duty. It's about beating the bounds at Aidensfield. I have to lead this year's perambulation on Ascension Day, with civic dignitaries. It's a very high profile police event, sir, the newspapers will be covering the story and it's a wonderful way of keeping the varied work of the police in the public eye. I must get things absolutely right on the day.'

I had known the superintendent when he was a mere inspector which meant I also knew the right tone of language to adopt as I did battle with his unspoken suspicions; clearly, he did not approve of me working at home. He thought I was involved in a form of duty dodging.

'How long will it take, Rhea? This reading of the file.'

'I don't know, sir, the file is about three inches thick and covers more than half a century of constables doing Aidensfield perambulations. I have to be the leader, sir, with about two hundred people following me so I need to get things right.'

'So what do you mean by that?'

'Once I've read the file, I have to submit my recommendations to Sergeant Blaketon and I am sure I will have to liaise with councillors, the clergy and the local school, so there's a lot of work to do and I think it will involve a lot of organizing.'

'Are you saying you might be office-bound for some time?'

'I'm saying, sir, that I need time to get things done properly and efficiently, especially as I shall be in full view of the public and the press. At this stage, I don't know how long it will take.'

'You could always work at Eltering Sub-Divisional Police Station, Rhea, there are spare offices there.'

'Sir, with all due respect, it will take half an hour and some expense to travel to Eltering. That is completely unnecessary because I have a telephone here and during the time I am in my office, I shall be within constant reach of the people who live and work on my beat. I cannot see the need to work anywhere else, especially nearly twenty miles away at Eltering.'

I wondered if my language was bordering on the insubordinate but he did not seem unduly fazed by my response.

'All right, Rhea, I take your points but don't think you can skive. And I shall expect to see that report you are submitting to Sergeant Blaketon.'

'I'll make sure you get a copy, sir.'

He rang off without wishing me good luck in my endeavours, but I knew he would instruct Sergeant Blaketon or perhaps Inspector Breckon from Eltering Sub-Division to visit my police house and check on me from time to time. The idea of a constable working at home was clearly troubling the superintendent. He might even decide to call upon a supervisory visit of his very own – a nice drive into the countryside around Aidensfield might be too appealing to ignore! But I would be ready for whoever called. As the children played therefore, I settled down to study the heavy file. Mary returned having enjoyed her brief break from the children and asked if I would be having lunch at home. I said I would and so I embarked on a comfortable day in my own little office albeit taking care not to be seen to be skiving from my duties. None of my supervisory officers called, although Sergeant Blaketon did ring once or twice, ostensibly to raise queries about other matters.

It proved to be a pleasant and interesting day's work, far from the onerous duty I was anticipating. I began to think Sergeant Blaketon had been winding me up in some way with his references to trouble and strife during the walk for the file revealed that the organization of the beating ceremony did not devolve upon me nor indeed upon any other individual. All those who took part made their own arrangements for Ascension Day with everyone assembling at the Aidensfield Oak at 10 a.m. They would then process together from that point. From the file, I learned that the participating parties would turn up without any prompting, sure to equip themselves with food and suitable clothing for a full day's walking. It dawned upon me that everyone had done the walk before and knew exactly what to do – all except me.

Study of the file also revealed I knew very little about the history and traditions of Aidensfield and district, several aspects of which were touched upon during the perambulation. That was something I decided to rectify as soon as possible because the area around Aidensfield seemed uncommonly rich with folklore, tradition, history and wild life in all its forms, amid spectacular countryside. My duties and family commitments had conspired to prevent any long-term exploration of the locality; now I could see why it was so popular with tourists and people with the necessary ample leisure time to fully enjoy it.

The huge, gnarled old tree known as the Aidensfield Oak was an outstanding example. It grew in the centre of the village green but its great age was uncertain because it appeared in records dating back more than 400 years. With a large expanse of common grassland around it, all beautifully tended by the constant munching of moorland sheep, it had always been a focus for local ceremonies and outdoor events. They included sports events, fairs, farm sales and annual customs such as those at New Year, Shrovetide, Easter, Midsummer Day, Michaelmas Day, Hallowe'en and Christmas. In between those events there may be maypole dancing, church services, agricultural shows, children's competitions and indeed any other event for which a focal point and a large area of well-cut level grassland were required. In former times, weddings had been conducted beneath such trees, then known as marriage oaks.

For my purpose, however, the oak was not part of the parish boundary. Other oaks, standing stones and distinctive landmarks were immovable points around the boundaries, but the Aidensfield Oak was merely the starting point. People assembled there at 10 a.m. on

Ascension Day and then moved to the first boundary marker, a tall, standing stone known as the Bracken Howe Stone. Some eight feet high and inclined slightly towards the east, it was about two miles away on an elevated part of the surrounding moorland and was visible for miles. It had been a parish boundary marker for as long as records had been kept.

From there, the boundary headed north-west along the summit of Bracken Rigg, across a marshy area of moorland and then into Ploatby Woods where Ploatby Beck flowed down from the marshy area to join Ashfordly Gill some distance downstream. At this point, the boundary did not pass along the bed of the beck but travelled as far as its junction with Ashfordly Gill, then turned south. For another mile or so the boundary followed a public footpath that skirted Lord Ashfordly's estate (much of his estate lay within Ashfordly parish).

The railway line formed the next stretch of the boundary as it headed south and I was surprised to find we had to walk through a short tunnel before crossing the line and heading over to the higher moors on the west. That was the most barren part of Aidensfield Parish with little more than open moorland, bogs and the sound of the curlew.

As the boundary headed west for about a mile, it crested a hill to turn south where it followed the route of an ancient dike, passed along the shores of a reservoir, headed through the cross passage of the Sheep Breeders' Arms and then wound its way before turning south-east to encircle the village. Along the route of the parish boundary were several old oak trees and lots of stone boundary markers, all to be thrashed with hazel rods. There seemed to be no specific time for completing the perambulation but it was clear that everyone went prepared with weather-proof clothing, food and maps. After all, Ascension Day was early in the year being the fortieth day after Easter and therefore celebrated on a moveable date, but always on a Thursday and, with rare exceptions, in May when the weather was unpredictable. It was known to the Anglicans as Holy Thursday which was the name Catholics gave to Maundy Thursday, i.e. the day before Good Friday. The fact that the Aidensfield Beating of the Bounds was celebrated on Ascension Day meant the churches took an active part – Catholics and Anglicans were represented in Aidensfield and I wondered whether the parish boundaries were those established before or after the Reformation. I hoped the respective priest and vicar would not fall out about the route!

From what I learned by reading the file, representatives of the churches, the parish council, the school, the Women's Institute and retired military personnel who were members of the British Legion all took an active part, although anyone else could join the fun. There appeared to be no order of precedence except for the constable at the front of the march and it seemed all I need worry about was the risk from motor vehicles whenever the large procession took to the roads. There was also the rumoured fracas that might develop at the Sheep Breeders' Arms but I began to wonder whether that was pure myth or whether the stories were based on a single incident long ago. I would find out on the day.

Using the file's list of contacts, I rang several to establish that my interpretation of events was correct and, with all my queries satisfactorily answered, I settled down to type my proposal for Sergeant Blaketon.

Using previous examples as my model, it was a simple document that set out to show that I knew the route, was known to the other participants and that I was capable of carrying out such a vital task. I could not understand why he had made such a fuss about it. I typed three copies of my proposal, one for Blaketon, one for the superintendent and one for myself, then placed the top two in clean envelopes and took them by motor bike to Ashfordly Police Station.

'That was quick!' said Alf Ventress when I walked in. 'I expected that task would occupy you for the whole day.'

'I can't see what the fuss is about,' I said. 'It's all very straightforward.'

'I'm glad you think so, Nick. Blaketon's out, he's gone to Eltering with the court files, so how about a cuppa?'

Having a cup of tea with Alf Ventress was always full of interest because he had such a wide knowledge of local affairs and a vast range of police experience upon which he could draw when coping with any incident, large or small. As we drank, he told me about some of his youthful escapades in the force and his words inevitably proffered good advice for young officers such as myself. I listened enthralled. As he chatted, I began to wonder whether he knew any more about the Aidensfield perambulation – perhaps he thought I knew more than I really did!

'Alf,' I said as he poured his third cup, 'this Beating the Bounds. Do you know anything about it, anything I should know?'

'Well, there's not a lot to know, Nick, it's all in that file. Or was it an earlier file I found in the loft? Do you know, I can't remember, but there is summat in those old files. Somebody wrote up the local history. . . .'

'Like what? Blaketon told me about possible trouble at the Sheep Breeders' Arms.'

'Oh that! Well, yes, it goes back years, Nick. I reckon folks still do battle about it even though few of 'em know why they're doing it or how long it's been going on. I think the real reason for the fuss has been lost in the passage of time but every three years, old wounds are reopened even though no one really knows what it's all about.'

'So what sort of battle are we talking about?'

'Young fellers on both sides. . . .'

'Both sides?' I asked.

'Aye, the Aidensfield side and the Gelderslackians both get themselves tanked up with ale in time for when the Aidensfield Beaters of the Bounds arrive. By then, they've all had a bit too much to drink – the Aidensfield lot carry their supplies with them – and the Gelderslackians have a go at the Aidensfield lads when they try to perambulate through the cross passage of the pub. They try to block the route. They will let you through, but when it comes to the others, the Aidensfielders respond, as you'd expect, and so a good old-fashioned pub brawl is the result. A few black eyes and bloody noses. Nothing worse. It's been going on for years, Nick. It's harmless, a bit of fun. No proceedings are ever instituted.'

'There's got to be a reason for it, Alf. If we can find that out, we might be able to stop the punch-up.'

'I don't think they want it stopped, Nick, it's become part of the tradition of Aidensfield's Beating the Bounds. People keep the practice going because it's always been done without anyone bothering to ask why.'

'So the fight has now developed into a custom all of its very own?'

'You could say so, yes. So I think my advice, Nick, is to leave well alone, let 'em battle it out on those moors as they've done for years. Even though it looks fairly serious it's not a real fight, more of a friendly boxing match without rules or gloves. They're all pals afterwards.'

'I find that a bit strange, but with your vast knowledge, do you know the reason for it?'

'Yes, as I said, it's in one of the files, probably one stored in the loft above us. I found a verse which goes:

At Ascension there'll be
A search so dark and so deep
For a treasure that only
A true man can keep.
Of jewels and bright gold
It's fit for a king
And. . . .

But the rest of the verse is missing, Nick.'

'Any idea what it means?'

'Aye, sort of. There's a tale that years ago, a rich man was staying at the Sheep Breeders' Arms when raiders struck. He had a fine cross around his neck, made of gold and jewels, and he managed to throw it down the well outside the pub before the thieves got hold of it. They never found it.'

'So where is it, Alf?'

'Still down the well, Nick, so they say. But later, one of the landlords heard the tale and thought he'd stop anyone searching the well – he'd searched it time and time again with no luck because it was so deep and the bottom was yards deep in mud. No one could find anything down there, let alone something as small as a necklet.'

'So how did he stop people from searching?'

'He built an extension to the pub, Nick. It stands right on top of that old well. He sealed it off; he reckoned if he couldn't have it, then no one else could. Lots have tried over the years, of course, digging up the floor and so on, but no one's found it. The well was filled in anyway. But, you see, the extension is in Aidensfield parish, not Gelderslack like the pub – so the story goes that each Ascension Thursday, the Gelderslackians protect the site from the Aidensfielders. You see, the old poem says there'll be a search at Ascension. It's been going on so long that everyone's forgotten the reason – and I doubt if many know the story of that sunken necklet. I reckon it's still there under that part of the pub and I suppose one day it might be found. Not in my time, I doubt.'

When Sergeant Blaketon read my proposal for coping with the perambulation he expressed satisfaction with my plans, and made arrangements to have extra officers at those points where the walking procession might cause danger to other road users. As advised, I took a back pack with my lunch, some folded waders and clothing suitable for any kind of Yorkshire weather and, of course, I was clad in my smartest uniform as befitting the office of Constable of Aidensfield.

The weather was kind to us and the schoolchildren were wonderful. They had been well briefed by the headmistress and galloped about joyously as they approached each of the boundary markers that they thoroughly lashed with their hazel sticks. In all, having waded through bogs, walked along river-beds, through tunnels, along main roads and across the moors it was a wonderful village event, full of fun and action but also with its serious element. Everyone involved would know where the parish boundaries were – including me.

When the procession, estimated to number around 120, approached the Sheep Breeders' Arms on its lofty moorland site, we could see a knot of young men waiting outside. This was the reception committee.

I was leading the way and it was clear that everyone in the Aidensfield group knew what to expect because the stragglers – about thirty young men from the village – detached themselves as the others strode forward to pass through the passage of the pub. I led the way to cheers from the Gelderslackians and everyone passed through without incident.

We all knew we must not attempt to enter the bar today. On Ascension Day, Aidensfielders must take their own refreshments outside. The rearguard then made their move.

I could not see what was going on because I, along with all the other peaceful travellers, was at the other side of the pub and so all we could do was listen to the shouting, hammering and thumping sounds. It sounded as though a battle of epic proportions was being waged and then, about fifteen minutes later, the gallant Aidensfielders straggled through the passage to cheers from their waiting colleagues. There were a few blackening eyes and bloody noses along with a torn garment or two, but nothing serious: no broken bones or major wounds. They were followed by their opponents for whom another mighty cheer arose whereupon the two warring factions shook hands, slapped backs and continued their friendship – until next Ascension Day.

As always, neither side had won but they'd had a mighty good battle and on Saturday would join each other once more to discuss the outcome over a few friendly pints of ale and a pork pie supper in the Sheep Breeders' Arms. I don't think anyone would try to find that mysterious missing jewel.

And so we all went home. We'd enjoyed a wonderful country walk in spectacular scenery, and the occasion produced a deep sense of friendship and unity among the villagers. Our purpose had been achieved and we all knew the extent of Aidensfield parish boundary.

I would make a positive report to Sergeant Blaketon in due course and it would join the thick file I had earlier used, but I did wonder whether I would still be the Aidensfield constable when the next perambulation took place.

Chapter 2

Homeward Bound

It is quite probable that in days of old the walking of Aidensfield's parish boundaries was the only occasion some of the residents actually left the village. Before the days of motor cars, trains and buses, travelling around the North York moors on foot or on horseback was a matter of hard necessity. Footpaths, trods, causeys and bridle-ways provided the shortest and most sensible routes to distant places but they were seldom used for leisure – except perhaps for a quiet bit of courting.

People didn't often travel for fun. They did so because it was necessary for commercial and social reasons and for ordinary, hardworking people holidays in far-off places were non-existent. They might be given a day off once a year at Christmas, or perhaps to attend a hiring fair if they were seeking work. Although in more recent times, wealthier people went on extended journeys to foreign parts, travelling overland or by sea on their grand tours, that luxury was beyond the means of most.

For centuries, farmers and smallholders from Aidensfield would trek the four miles or so into Ashfordly to sell their wares at the weekly market and that was perhaps their only day away from working the land. It meant they could sit in one of the ale houses and swap yarns although they never forgot that such a day was for business rather than mere fun. Many hard bargains resulted and such days were long and hard with an early start and a late finish. It was both worthwhile and enjoyable because deals were done and useful contacts established.

Shoppers also made good use of the market to buy their food, clothing, crafts and other goods. Market-days were therefore one occasion when the people left their homes for an outing, even if it meant walking four miles to town and four miles back again, carrying heavy baskets.

The notion of travelling overseas was something aspired to only by the rich, or perhaps the very adventurous. Nonetheless, some young men were influenced by stirring tales of others running off to sea. In the early seventeenth century a lad from my home village joined a ship at Whitby and found himself fighting the Spanish Armada, later becoming a highly successful pirate and eventually a very wealthy and respected citizen. His name was Tom Ferris who became Lord Mayor of Hull and Warden of Trinity House. A pack-horse bridge in Glaisdale was rebuilt by him in 1619 to the memory of his wife, a lass from that village. Another lad from the moors was James Cook who went to sea to become the great navigator, explorer and seaman who discovered Australia. Exploits of that kind caused others to yearn for a better and more exciting life overseas, but the likelihood of them emulating such heroes was seldom converted into reality.

In the nineteenth and early twentieth centuries, though, farmers and smallholders from the North York Moors listened to tales of the wealth and happiness that could be found by farming overseas, Canada being a much-quoted example. Many tenant farmers struggled to make a living from the bleak Yorkshire moorlands, sometimes paying a high proportion of their income in rent. With unpredictable and severe weather adding to their problems, many existed literally on the breadline. Once their expenses were paid, there was very little left to live on and certainly nothing for luxuries like fine clothes or holidays.

Some were impressed by the stirring tales of families in similar circumstances who had found the means and courage to emigrate to Canada, Australia or New Zealand, there to start new lives. Such tales were commonplace even in the early years of the twentieth century. Inevitably, all such stories were about successful ventures – the people back home rarely heard about the failures and indeed, some stubborn Yorkshire folk would never admit a failure. Even if things were difficult, they'd send uplifting letters to their families at home. The abiding image, therefore, was one of constant success for those who were brave enough to make that massive emotional break with family tradition and local expectations.

One advantage of a farmer's enterprise overseas was that he could actually become the owner of the land he farmed instead of paying rent for it – in far off countries, land was there for the taking. All you had to do was make the journey and settle and register a piece of unclaimed land. Many did so and built their own houses, perhaps using wood if they'd gone to Canada. In that way they became land and property owners, something they could seldom hope to achieve in England.

Letters from those who had achieved that break were avidly read in their home country persuading many young and ambitious moorland farmers to cross the seas to begin new and successful lives. Many married their sweethearts and took them overseas, often to the envy of those left behind in their tough unproductive homeland as tenants on big estates. Indeed, some of my own ancestors from the moors went to Canada in search of their fortunes and, as they never returned, we assumed they had been successful.

One such family was called Corby whose members farmed high on the moors above Shelvingby. They were perhaps slightly different from their contemporaries because they owned their house and the land upon which it stood, that wise purchase having being made centuries earlier by an enterprising Corby when the local estate was facing hard times during the Civil War. Thus they were landowners, not tenants. Such small landowners became known as yeomen – they owned the land, but worked upon it beside their labourers, unlike members of the aristocracy who paid others to work for them.

The family home of the Corby family was called Brockrigg Heights. It was a splendid and rather rugged stone-built two-storey house with a range of sturdy farm buildings and a spread of several hundred acres, much of which was open moorland inhabited by their flock of hardy black-faced sheep.

The place was surrounded by open views of a treeless, heather-clad landscape with bracken, boulders and babbling brooks stretching for miles. For the hikers who often passed by, it seemed an idyllic location, but when trying to make a decent living from such a place, it could become hell on earth, especially in winter when the snow could be eight or ten feet deep (3m or more) with drifts three times as high. Plans to survive such winters were made as early as August and September by building up stocks of food and fuel, along with animal bedding and fodder, sufficient to last until February, March or even later.

When I arrived in Aidensfield as the village constable, one of my first tasks was to become acquainted with the local farmers and their families. Rural constables had many dealings with them – for example, every quarter we had to check the farmers' livestock registers. In addition there were duties under the Diseases of Animals Act of 1950 along with constant concern about sheep worrying by dogs, the enforcement of regulations about the transit of animals, and various laws governing horses and the slaughter of animals. There was also the regular inspection of firearms, their licences and certificates. And, of course, there was a crime prevention element, persuading farmers to safeguard from thieves all their expensive equipment, livestock and isolated homes.

Soon after arriving at Aidensfield, I checked the address list of the livestock registers on my beat and saw that Brockrigg Heights was on the very edge of my patch, several miles from Aidensfield. It was isolated high up on the moors and was certainly not the sort of place you'd pop into when passing by. It meant a trek of a mile and a half from a rough unsurfaced green lane which itself was two miles from another very rough country track that eventually entered a surfaced rural lane. In all, the spread lay about five miles from Shelvingby, its nearest village, and it was totally alone, its nearest neighbour being more than a mile away.

Quite clearly, a visit to Brockrigg Heights would have to wait until I had a sound reason for calling – perhaps for the renewal of a firearms certificate. As that duty came around only once every three years, however, I thought a quarterly visit to check the stock register might appear to be a better reason – and that small task was something I could not ignore. Sergeant Blaketon would surely badger me to get my records updated. As I had not checked the Corbys' registers since arriving in Aidensfield almost three months earlier, the time had now come when I had no choice but to conclude that minor piece of business. One Tuesday morning, therefore, I prepared for the trip on my trusty little Francis Barnett motor bike, hoping it would cope with the rough terrain.

Happily, it was a mild day in early autumn with the heather in full bloom producing an unrivalled carpet of purple stretching from horizon to horizon. There was the occasional white patch that was a grazing sheep, or dark patch where the heather had been burned off earlier in the year to promote new growth. As I chugged along, I marvelled at the sheer beauty of the unspoilt landscape, congratulating myself for being lucky enough to live and work in such magnificent surroundings. People paid good money to come and visit those moors. They came for walks and sight-seeing; some paid huge sums for the privilege of shooting grouse, an event necessary to save both the grouse and the heather. Grouse cannot exist without the heather, but too many grouse result in a lack of food for the birds and so they become vulnerable to a disease from which they die. Helping nature in this respect – cultivating the heather and culling the birds – is a delicate but necessary operation. Not only that, it creates a valuable income from the moors that in turn results in rural employment.

Eventually after a very bumpy ride I reached the gate marked Brockrigg Heights and happily it was standing open. Opening a gate whilst in charge of a motor bike is never easy! I chugged through, noting the empty fields amid the sea of surrounding heather. Cresting a rise, I saw in the distance the clutch of farm buildings with the fine stone house among them; the outbuildings were rather like a brood of chickens surrounding a mother hen, but their purpose was to shelter the house – to such farmers splendid views were not important. They concentrated upon protecting the wintering animals from the worst of the weather, even though most of the livestock would be under cover. The tough black-faced sheep wouldn't be sheltered – they remained on the moors throughout the worst of the winter. Cattle, horses, pigs and hens would all be enclosed.

As I rode on with great care due to the rough track across the fields, the place seemed deserted. It was not yet winter – the cattle should have been in the fields and the poultry should have been pecking at the ground around the buildings. And there was no smoke from the chimneys. I eased the bike towards the gate that opened into the fold yard more and more certain the place was deserted – quite literally there was no sign of life, neither animal nor human, but I stopped inside the complex of buildings and parked my machine. It was evident the large oblong yard had not been used for a long time – there were no footmarks, no fresh animal dung, no midden heaps, no tractors awaiting attention, no ploughs in need of a cleaning session and no hens pecking in the dirt. Leaving my helmet on the seat of the bike, I began to walk around, checking all the byres and stables, pig sties and hen houses, but there was nothing. All were empty.

The house looked deserted too – the windows and outer paint-work were dirty and there were cobwebs around the back door, all adding to the overall appearance of neglect. There was hay and straw in the outbuildings, and some contained machinery such as a tractor, a binder, various horse-drawn vehicles and ploughs and even an old Austin car.

Somewhat apprehensively, I made my way to the back door, not knowing what I might find – front doors of farms and rural houses in this region were rarely used except for weddings and funerals. When I reached it I looked through the kitchen window. There was a huge table and chairs all around it, and places set with plates, mugs, knives and forks. Three settings, I noticed. The kitchen units were also full of crockery and kitchen utensils. So the place was occupied!

I hammered on the door and waited. Nothing.

I tried again and again, using my fists to rattle the door, but there was no response. I walked around the house, peering through its ground-floor windows to see that it was fully furnished − a comfortable lounge had easy chairs and a settee, whilst the dining-room had a splendid oak table with matching chairs and sideboard. I banged on the front door for a while, again with no response, and then returned to the back. This time I tried the brass door knob. Surprisingly, the big door swung open.

This time I shouted, 'Hello, anyone there?'

There was no reply. I ventured further inside, shouting all the time and announcing my identity. Nothing. Not a sound.

I realized I had not checked on who should be living here, except their surname was Corby; I did not know whether there was a Mr and Mrs Corby, or merely one person perhaps retired, or a family with children. . . .

'Mr Corby?' I cupped my hands around my mouth and bellowed through the kitchen into the spacious hall, but there was no response. 'Hello, it's PC Rhea from Aidensfield.'

I wandered around the ground-floor rooms, shouting all the time and peering into cupboards and the pantry, but all to no avail. I began to wonder if something dreadful had happened – a fatality of some kind perhaps, an accidental shooting, a sudden death through illness. . . ? The entire spectrum of likely causes of sudden death flooded into my mind as I toured the house, calling and examining likely hiding places. But I found nothing.

Then it was time to go upstairs. It was a big house and I guessed it would have six or even more large bedrooms. Such farmhouses were spacious because, even until the early years of the twentieth century, the farm workers – male and female – lived in. They had a separate staircase and would generally share bedrooms, men in one part of the house and girls in another – but they were fed by the farmer's wife who also did their laundry; indeed, they took their meals with the family.

My tour of the ten bedrooms produced nothing. Every room was furnished with a bed neatly made, and the main room had a double bed, also neatly made. I searched every bed, turning back the covers and peering underneath, but found no one, dead or alive. The wardrobes were checked too, as was the bathroom and loft. Nothing suspicious. Although the house was deserted, everything appeared ready for the return of its owners although I noticed there were no stocks of fresh food, just a few tins of beans and soup. Even the fires were laid ready to be ignited. I shouted and called again and again, double-checking my earlier search and then went outside.

I repeated my shouting and searching in the outbuildings, checking the hay loft, the pig sties, the stables and cow byres, but everything was deserted. There were no people and no livestock of any kind. And yet the house was not locked. Few rural people ever did lock their back doors and regular visitors often went in without invitation, shouting to announce their presence. By contrast, the front door was always locked.

People such as visiting priests, police officers, postmen, doctors and nurses, vets, Ministry of Agriculture officials, meter readers, pools collectors, insurance men, casual workmen, relations, friends and neighbours would all open the back door and shout, 'It's only me.' Quite literally, it was always open house on such farms.

The discovery of this vast empty but furnished house left me in something of a dilemma. The house and its contents were in good condition albeit a bit dusty, so had something dreadful happened? If so, why hadn't the alarm been raised? If the Corby family had vanished without explanation, surely someone would have alerted me or some other responsible person such as the local priest or doctor. But if the family had left the farm, why was all their furniture still in position with the beds ready made and the back door unlocked? The fact that all the animals were absent with their quarters quite clean suggested the absence had been planned over an extended period, but the presence of the furnishings inside the house indicated a possible return. Or was this an involuntary and even forced absence? Had the family been murdered and their livestock stolen?

The more I pondered the question, the more puzzling it became, so I thought I had better make enquiries in an attempt to establish what had happened. But because there

were no houses anywhere near this farm, I decided to call
in the village of Shelvingby to begin my questioning. Surely
someone there would know.

On the long return trip to civilization, I was fortunate to
meet one of the local farmers slowly driving his tractor out
of Shelvingby. It was a surfaced road beyond the village
and I waved him to a stop, managing to hoist my motor
bike onto its stand on the tarmac road surface as I talked to
him. I could see the worried look on his face as I
approached. His name was Josh Simpson.

'Now then Mr Simpson,' I greeted him as he stared at
me. I wondered if he was doing something illegal because
his old face bore a very worried expression. 'I wondered if
you could help me.'

'Help? Oh, aye, Ah thought thoo was stopping me for
doing summat unlawful. A speed check mebbe.' And his
expression relaxed with a smile at his own little joke.

'I'm sure you wouldn't do anything unlawful, Mr
Simpson,' I smiled. He was a stout, grizzled man of about
sixty-five and he sported several days' growth of whiskers
beneath a flat cap that appeared to have been used
variously as a duster, polishing rag and cleaning cloth. I had
never seen him without that cap and knew him from earlier
visits to his farm on the outskirts of Shelvingby – he
specialized in saddleback pigs and I had issued many
movement licences for him.

'Nothing that Ah'd let on.' He grinned. 'So what can Ah
do for you, Constable Rhea?' He did not climb down from
his tractor and kept the engine running – perhaps the
battery was low and it was difficult to start once stopped.

'It's about Brockrigg Heights,' I shouted, above the noise of the engine. 'I've just been up there and the place is deserted.'

'Aye, it is.' He nodded furiously without further explanation.

'So where are they? The Corby family?'

'They've gone out,' he said.

'Yes, I can see that, but the place is still full of furniture and the door's not locked; they seem to have gone for a long time.'

'It's left as it is in case they come back.' He nodded again as if in agreement with himself.

'Come back?' I puzzled. 'So where have they gone?'

'Canada,' he grinned.

'Canada? For a holiday you mean?'

'Holiday? Folks like us don't take holidays, Mr Rhea. Nay, they've gone to find work. To get a better life. There's not a lot o' profit in sheep nowadays.'

'But if they've emigrated, surely they would have emptied the house and sold it?'

'Not them, Mr Rhea, not them lads. Nay, they back things both ways. They've left t'house as it is in case they want to come back.'

'I thought they'd gone to start a new life?'

'Aye, they 'ave. But there's no point in taking all that furniture to Canada, and then havin' to turn round and fetch it back again if things don't work out as expected. And if they do come back, they'll want somewhere to live, eh? They wouldn't want to start all over again, messing about looking for a house to buy or rent when they've already got one.'

'So they just packed their suitcases and went?'

'Aye, about two year back after selling t'stock. That would give 'em enough cash to buy summat over yonder and set up as farmers.'

'So we might never know how they're doing, will we? Or whether they might come back?'

'Nay, they'd never say, but if things don't work out as expected, they'll just come back 'ere and start afresh. That awd house won't take any harm being empty, Mr Rhea, it was built to last.'

'So who's gone to Canada? I don't know the family.'

'All of 'em,' was his reply.

'I mean, is it mother and father, sons, daughters, or what?'

'Oh, aye, Ah see what you mean. Nay, it's t'three lads, Mr Rhea. Brothers, they are. Triplets in fact, Bill, Ben and Bernie. Their awd folks died some years back, leaving t'farm to t'three lads.'

'So how old are they?'

'Dunno, in their forties, Ah'd say. Not young lads and not awd fellers, summat in between.'

'Are they married?'

'Not them! They ain't time to get wed, Mr Rhea, not when running a farm like Brockrigg Heights. They never got out to meet lasses, and besides, what lass in her right mind would want to live up yonder?'

'Right, thanks for this, Mr Simpson. You've been most helpful. I'll amend my records and make sure I call here once in a while, just to keep an eye on the place.'

'Don't you worry about that awd house, Mr Rhea. Those of us farming in these parts will keep an eye on things and we might even use them outbuildings for our own cattle and pigs if t'weather turns really bad. And we'll light a fire or two to keep t'spot aired i' winter. Them lads know t'house will be fit for 'em to come back to if things don't work out as expected. But they've been away summat like two years, so things must be going well for 'em.'

I had discovered all I wanted to know and so, after some banter about local happenings in Shelvingby, I thanked him and continued my journey.

Now I could bring my records up to date, and I had even managed to get the forenames of the owners of Brockrigg Heights. They were three hard-working young men who had gone abroad to seek their fortunes; they would not be the first and they would not be the last to make such an effort to improve their lives. As the months and years passed during my tour of duty at Aidensfield, the situation at Brockrigg Heights slowly receded as part of my ongoing duties.

Nonetheless, I remained aware of the vast empty house on the moors and paid the occasional visit just to ensure it had not been taken over by squatters, vandalized by mischievous youngsters, or used by ramblers as a place of shelter in which to sleep and eat. I knew that Farmer Simpson and his colleagues from Shelvingby would also be keeping an eye on the premises and if there was a problem of the sort that involved the police, I knew Josh would inform me.

It would be about three years after my arrival at

Aidensfield that the phone rang and when I answered, I detected the faint hint of a Canadian accent in the man's voice.

'PC Rhea, Aidensfield,' I responded.

'Can I come and see you, Mr Rhea,' said the voice. 'I need to get some firearms certificates sorted out.'

'Yes, of course. You say "some" certificates? You need only one, you know, all your weapons will be listed on it.'

'Yes, but there's three of us, all with our own rifles and shotguns.'

'Oh, right. Well, in that case I could come and see you if that would make things easier, especially if three of you are involved.'

'Would you? That would be a great help; we are rather isolated.'

'So who's calling?'

'My name is Bill Corby,' he said with the Canadian accent sounding stronger. 'From Brockrigg Heights above Shelvingby.'

It took a few moments for the significance of his words to register in my mind and then I realized who he was.

'Oh, I know the place,' I said. 'And I recognize the name. I thought you'd gone to Canada?'

'We did,' he said. 'And now we've come back.'

'All of you?' I asked.

'Yes, all of us,' was his reply.

'Right,' I said. 'I'll come along to introduce myself. It would be nice to meet you all. How about tomorrow afternoon? Three o'clock or so?'

'Fine, Mr Rhea, and we'll make sure the kettle is on.'

And so it was that I made that long motor bike trek back to Brockrigg Heights, this time knowing the splendid house would be occupied. I had placed a few firearms certificate application forms in my panniers and would also update the Corbys on the current situation so far as Diseases of Animals legislation and procedures were concerned, along with any other relevant changes to the law as it affected farmers.

There would also be the matter of British driving licences to consider and probably lots of other queries. I would do my best to help them re-settle into their former home.

As I rode towards the farm things did not appear to have altered since my previous visit, but when I was crossing the field on my way to the actual buildings, some changes were evident. For one thing, smoke was rising from two of the chimneys and, when I approached the entrance to the fold yard, I could see a line of washing fluttering in the moorland breeze. At least three cars were parked in the yard too, and upstairs I could see the windows were open and curtains were flapping in the wind. The old house had come back to life, and I felt a glow of pleasure – I hated to see wonderful old buildings being allowed to deteriorate through lack of care. As I chugged into the yard, a golden retriever came out to greet me, wagging its feathered tail and seeming to smile as only retrievers seem able to do. I parked the bike, removed my crash helmet and drew the file of papers from my pannier, then strode towards the back door.

A man opened it before I knocked; he was relaxed, tall

and handsome with broad shoulders, a mop of unruly fair hair, blue eyes and a ready smile. And he was clean shaven. I estimated his age as being around the mid-forties.

'You must be PC Rhea,' he said. 'I'm Bill Corby, I rang you.' And he held out his hand for me to shake. I did so; it was a firm grip and I found myself instantly warming to this man.

He seemed more like a city businessman than a Yorkshire farmer. I wondered if that was the result of his brief spell of work in Canada.

'Hello, nice to meet you. I see you've brought this place back to life already.'

'This old house is indestructible, Mr Rhea. It's a bit like a smouldering fire – you give a stir with a poker and it comes back to life in a flash. You'd never guess we'd been away from here for about five years. We've given it a bit of stir and it's come back to life.'

'I was worried about you leaving it unlocked.'

'I can never remember that back door ever being locked,' he said. 'My mum and dad, and my grandparents before them, always said we should be open at all times to take in folks who might need rest and refreshment. It's a long tradition of this farm, seeing as it's standing in such a remote place.'

'You're very trusting.'

'That's the way things are,' was his reply. By now we were entering the spacious kitchen. I could see it had been thoroughly dusted and cleaned with an Aga cooker warming the air as a kettle sang on one of its rings.

'Come through to the parlour,' he invited and I followed.

'We're all through there; you must meet the whole family and then we can get down to business. You'll have a cup of tea and a slice of fruit cake?'

'I'd love to.'

I followed him into the room he called the parlour and found it full of people. Or it seemed to be full at first glance. In fact there were five in addition to Bill and me. They were sitting in the wonderful old leather armchairs around a blazing log fire. A small coffee table was laid out with dainty cups and plates, along with a milk jug, sugar basin and plate of sliced fruit cake. But what puzzled me was that there were three women, all mirror images of one another whilst the two other men looked just like Bill. I knew they were his brothers. All of them rose to their feet as I entered the room.

'This is PC Rhea from Aidensfield, our local bobby,' he introduced me. 'Now, Mr Rhea, that chap at the back on the left is my brother Benjamin, Ben for short and the other one is Bernard, Bernie for short. I'm William as you might have guessed, or Bill to my friends. I don't need to tell you we're triplets, not quite identical but very nearly so.'

'Yes, I knew that from local knowledge,' I acknowledged.

'Now, these ladies are our wives. Jane, Joan and Jenny.' And he pointed to each one. All were beautiful women with long black hair, dark eyes and sun-tanned skins, and all were about the same age as the brothers. And they all looked identical.

One of them smiled and said, 'We're triplets as well, PC Rhea, we met in Toronto so everyone's going to have fun working out whose wife is who. I'm Jane, the eldest by twenty minutes. Bill's wife.'

'Right,' I said, 'Nice to meet you, but I don't know Toronto!'

'It used to be called York, and its new name of Toronto, dating from 1834, means place of meeting in the language of the American Indians. And that's where we all met. Strange, eh?'

'Thanks, we all learn something every day!'

'We couldn't wait to see England,' said another of the women. 'We'd heard so much about it we thought we should come here to start a new life.'

'We went to Canada to start afresh but here we are back home – and it's good to see the old spot again,' said Bill. 'We're going to reconstruct this farm as a hotel, Mr Rhea, the girls' background is within the hotel industry and they see great potential here. Transform the outbuildings into luxury bedrooms, build log cabins for the hardy types such as hikers and ramblers – we might even consider a ski slope. These lasses know how to cope with snow. And we will build a large room for banquets, improve access to the whole place, bring the house up-to-date with central heating and so on, and have our individual apartments. And out here, of course, we're not going to disturb anyone with loud music or fireworks. Anyway, those are our plans, we've sold everything in Canada.'

'Except our little hotel,' smiled the third of the women. 'We're keeping that in case we change our minds.'

'And with that, I think we should all sit down to enjoy our cake and tea, then afterwards we can discuss firearms with PC Rhea. The girls have always said how they'd like to meet a real English bobby.'

As I began to open my file of forms, I wondered just how long they would remain at Brockrigg Heights but their plans sounded feasible as Bill said, 'Let's start with that nice cup of English tea and cake, shall we?'

Chapter 3

Well, I'll Be Bound!
Money For Old Rope

Within the realm of criminal law, there is a Latin saying that reads: *De minimus non curat lex.* One simple interpretation is: 'The law does not concern itself with trifles' and because jokers often wonder why our legal system is not interested in puddings, sweets and assorted delicacies, the saying is often quoted as 'The law does not concern itself with trifling matters.' That makes much more sense to many more people.

I think the purpose of this judicial wisdom was to place some kind of advisory restraint upon over-zealous officials such as police officers, customs officials, lawyers, income tax inspectors, parking officials, council employees and anyone else whose duty is to enforce the law or other regulations. When I was undergoing my basic police training, I was made aware of this advice because we were told that police officers had wide powers of discretion as to how and when the law was enforced. The wise use of that discretion is vital – without it, we would degenerate into a police state. In other words, we did not have to enforce the *letter* of the law, but more importantly, we had to apply the *spirit* of the law. And there is a significant difference between the two.

Many members of the public can quote examples where officials have enforced various rules and regulations to the point of rigid absurdity and perhaps stupidity, but a police officer needs an instinctive wisdom as to when and how to use his or her wide powers of discretion.

Those powers are *not* to be used to encourage law breaking, the bending of various rules or the concealment of breaches of the law when friends are involved – that is not the point. They should be exercised in a way that encourages the public to respect the law and those who enforce it.

Powers of discretion have now been largely destroyed by machines such as parking meters, closed-circuit television cameras and speed cameras where no discretion is permitted. Similarly, councils are being given greater powers to fine people for not putting out their wheelie bins correctly or similar misdemeanours. The latter changes are a very worrying authoritarian trend.

So far as mechanical devices are concerned, a machine or camera tells you that you have committed an offence even if you are a mere fraction over the allotted time, or that you jumped the traffic lights on amber by a fraction of a second, or that you exceeded the prevailing speed limit by a mere one or two miles per hour. The imposition of targets, so beloved of governments, also encourages the law to be enforced by the letter – people are prosecuted merely so that targets are met, not because their behaviour or minor breach of some regulation justifies an arrest or summons.

It follows that in the good old days when police officers patrolled their beats with pride, it was widely accepted that they would not enforce the law if it involved a trifling kind of infringement. For example, if a bobby spotted a car driving at 32 m.p.h. in a 30 m.p.h restricted area, he would probably ignore it (unless it was being driven carelessly or had been stolen). He would ignore it until it reached 35 m.p.h.; any speed between 35 m.p.h. and 40 m.p.h. might justify stopping the car to caution the driver about his actions, but at those kinds of speeds, a prosecution was unlikely.

However, speeding at more than 40 m.p.h. in a 30 m.p.h. restricted area was likely to attract a summons. Certainly, any case of reckless, dangerous or careless driving at whatever speed would result in a prosecution – and we should not forget that people can drive carelessly at 5 m.p.h. In the past, the police recognized that fast driving in itself is not dangerous – to become dangerous it requires other salient factors. I recall one traffic officer saying that driving at 70 m.p.h. on an open road in dry conditions and with no other vehicle in sight was not dangerous, even if the limit was 50 m.p.h. He could be breaking the speed limit but not driving dangerously. However, driving on a motorway with a 70 m.p.h. limit and achieving that speed in thick fog and icy conditions would be dangerous, even if the speed limit was not being broken. Similarly, a speeding offence on a busy street full of children and adults in the middle of the afternoon would be dangerous, but not so if it occurred at three o'clock on a morning in a deserted part of town. It is always hoped that common sense will prevail, something speed cameras do not take into account.

Sadly, some police officers and other officials are not blessed with either common sense or an ability to exercise discretion – they enforce the law precisely as it is written down in the statute or rule book and, in so doing, cause immense damage and harm to themselves, the public and the police service.

I recall a colleague, a senior motor patrol driver who was on night duty in a busy urban area. His non-driving observer was a young constable, straight out of training school and eager to catch his first offender. As the two were cruising through a deserted part of the town at 3.30 a.m. a modest old banger hurtled into view from a side street and began its rapid journey along the main thoroughfare leading out of town.

'A speeder!' cried the rookie constable. 'Let's get him.'

'Right,' said the senior constable, accelerating in the wake of the rapidly departing vehicle. It was doing 60 m.p.h. on a 30 m.p.h. restricted road and they caught it very quickly, pulling it into a lay-by. Out leapt the rookie constable complete with notebook at the ready and he ran to the driver's door while the older copper walked sedately to the back of the car and looked inside. On the back seat was a distressed young woman clearly in the advanced stages of labour.

So focused was he upon booking the driver, the young bobby had not noticed the drama inside the rear of the vehicle which was now in darkness. He promptly set about telling the driver in no uncertain tones that he had exceeded the speed limit, gone through two sets of traffic lights at red and probably was driving dangerously as well. Furthermore, he wanted to inspect the hapless man's driving licence, insurance, MOT certificate and road tax disc; then there was likely to be a question of testing his brakes, lights and steering. As the youthful driver was doing his best to explain the urgency of his mission the young copper ignored him, thinking he was making up excuses, then his senior colleague arrived at the driver's door. All this took merely a couple of minutes.

'Stand back, Geoff,' he said abruptly to the rookie.

He then spoke to the distraught driver. 'You know where the hospital is?'

'No, not really. I know it's up here somewhere,' he said. 'Sorry I was speeding but I have to get her there . . . she's due any minute and she's got a blood disorder.'

'Right, follow me. How fast will your car go? Safely, I mean!'

'A good sixty, sixty-five.'

'Right, follow me. Keep as close as you can – we'll jump all the red lights and I'll put my blue flashers on. . . .'

And so the high-speed procession began with the old banger doing its best to maintain contact with the high performance police car, but they arrived at the hospital in time for the young woman to be admitted. She gave birth a few minutes after admission and the right treatment for her blood disorder was made readily available. The experienced police officer also parked the couple's car for them, leaving the keys at the hospital's reception desk. It was a good night's police work – and, hopefully, a lesson for a rookie constable. I was reminded that it was Shakespeare who wrote, 'The better part of valour is discretion.'

Many police officers can tell horror stories of their colleagues enforcing trivial breaches of the law – drinking late in a pub by only two minutes over time, over-staying on a parking restricted area by a couple of minutes, failing to sign a driving licence (a popular offence among rule-bound officers), failing to properly record the contents of a sack of coal, sounding a car horn while the vehicle was stationary, flying a kite in the street, making a slide on ice in the street – and there are countless other examples. In many cases, it was impossible to deter these rule-bound bobbies from this kind of oppressive behaviour because their reply was always, 'It's the law – these people are breaking the law. It's written down in black and white.' In these cases, it requires a good and wise sergeant to explain the difference between prosecution and persecution.

Inevitably, however, further questions arise. How far can we take the idea of the law not concerning itself with trifling matters? What is trifling to one person might be considered very serious by another. Is it a matter of personal opinion or are there precedents?

Suppose a police officer arrested a thief for stealing something worth only a few pence or even something quite valueless. Would his actions – and all the subsequent paperwork – be justified? It must be said that if such a crime had been reported officially to the police, then it would become their duty to enquire into the crime and, if necessary, apprehend the offender, irrespective of the value of the stolen property. After all, a crime is a crime irrespective of the value of the stolen goods and it is true that some objects have little or no financial worth but they might be of great sentimental value and importance to the owner. It is almost impossible to put a price on a truly beloved object, but is there a lower limit of a property's value at which the police should not take any action? Can theft, vandalism or damage ever be considered too trifling for the police to concern themselves?

Should the law ignore such occurrences even if they are crimes and, if so,where does one draw the line about, say, the value of the stolen object or the nuisance level which has led to a complaint? Here are two examples.

Bob Farrow of Bay Tree Farm, Elsinby was an old-fashioned Yorkshire farmer who, throughout his working life, had struggled to earn a living on his modest spread. He kept a small herd of dairy cattle, and a flock of sheep that ran on the distant moor, whilst around the farmyard in the village there were always a few hens, ducks and geese. He also grew potatoes and swedes. In his mid-seventies, he was far from wealthy but, because the farm was rented, he could not afford to retire completely.

His rent was cheap, little more than it had been at the outset of World War I when his father was tenant, and so he could scrape a living for himself and his wife, Annie –

enough to pay the rent, then feed and clothe themselves.

The low rental was reflected in the condition of the farm – it had no indoor toilet, for example. There was no hot water upstairs, no bathroom, no central heating and a very primitive electrical system. The couples' hot water came from a back boiler fitted with a brass tap that poured heated hot water from a fireside reservoir into a bucket. A bath – a rare event indeed – was taken in an old tin tub placed before the kitchen fire on bath night (Friday) when the old couple took weekly turns at being first into the shallow clean water.

I think they shared the water but didn't bathe together! Both were quite stocky and I doubt if they could have fitted together into the old tin tub. Whilst bathing, they locked the doors and closed the curtains, and most of us around the village knew when it was bath night at Bay Tree Farm. The tin bath, which normally hung on a wall outside the back kitchen, would disappear – and people knew it was in the kitchen being put to very good use. They bathed on a Friday night because it was traditional to do so, but also because they both went into Malton on a Saturday morning to visit the market and they wanted to look their best on this weekly outing.

Bob was a sturdy individual about five feet ten inches tall and had probably been a powerful man in his youth, the sort who could toss a sack of corn around as if it was a bag of sweets. Once a good cricketer for Elsinby, he was now semi-retired but retained a keen interest in the local team with Annie helping with the cricket teas. They had one son who lived away; he had rejected farming as a career and, I believe, had joined the army with lots of service overseas which explained why he seldom came home. Bob and Annie now worked at just enough pace to fund their quiet, peaceful and unadventurous way of life.

And then one day Bob had a theft to report. He hailed me as I was carrying out a foot patrol around Elsinby and said, 'Nick, a word if I may.'

He was in the farmyard swilling caked mud from his tractor when he spotted me, but his shouting and waving of arms readily attracted my attention. I let myself in through the main farm gate, the one that opened on to the street. It swung shut beneath its own weight as I strode across to talk to him. Annie, from the kitchen, had noticed my arrival and shouted from the doorstep, 'The kettle's on, Mr Rhea, and I've made some lovely apple pie . . . there's some fresh cream an' all. You must come in for a taste.'

'Aye,' Bob called in response. 'In just a minute, our Annie.' Then before continuing our discussion over the pie and cream, he said to me, 'Nick, do you ken owt different about this farmyard?'

I glanced around as I wondered if I'd omitted to notice a new car or tractor, or some impressive kind of agricultural machinery. There might even be a new roof on the dairy, or had he got around to repairing that window in the cow byre? It had been broken ever since I was posted to Aidensfield – and it was still broken. When I glanced around, I noticed nothing out of the ordinary.

'Sorry, Bob, no. It all looks the same to me.'

'Aye,' he said. 'That's t'trouble. It allus looks t'same – I never even noticed it had gone. It's only when you come to want to use it and it's not there, that you miss it. Like this morning. I went for it and it had gone. I can't say when it vanished, but it has vanished for sure, clean as a whistle.'

'What has?'

'That bit o' rope I use for holding t'gate open.'

'Bit of rope?' I puzzled.

'Aye, it's allus hung on a nail on t'cowshed wall. For years, it's hung there, under a little corrugated iron roof to keep rain off.'

He pointed to the place in question and I could see the miniature roof, but no rope.

'It's fairly close to the road, Nick – I reckon somebody's come past and nicked it. But who'd want my piece o' rope? Mebbe they wanted a tow rope? Now that could be t'answer . . . somebody nicking it for a tow rope.'

I was trying to recollect seeing the piece of rope in question but despite my struggle to visualize it in place, I could not bring it to mind. I had never noticed the rope in its home location, consequently, I had no idea which piece of rope Bob was talking about.

'Are you chaps coming in or not?' that was Annie shouting from the kitchen step.

'Aye, now we've done our business,' grunted Bob.

'We've not quite finished, Bob, I'll need to ask you some more questions,' I told him, as he walked towards the kitchen. 'For my crime report.'

'You'll never catch t'thief,' he grunted. 'Not now. He'll be miles away. And my rope with 'im, towing summat happen as not. I can't see t'need to make a fuss, not now. It's too late.'

'Whenever we get a formal report of a crime, Bob, we have to make an official record of it. It's allocated a crime number in case you want to claim from your insurance—'

'Insurance? For that bit o' rope? I wouldn't say it's worth owt, not even a farthing, or a ha'penny, so there's no point in making a claim.'

'But if it's important enough to report to me that it's gone missing, then it must have some value, Bob.'

'Aye, but not monetary worth, Nick. Usefulness. That's the most useful piece of rope I've ever had. My dad used it when he lived here, and I've used it ever since I took over. You're talking half a century or more of using that bit o' rope.'

'So it must have been extremely useful,' I said, following him into the kitchen where I could smell freshly baked apple pie. The large oak table was set out with mugs, plates and spoons even though it was neither lunchtime nor teatime. I wasn't sure what sort of break this might be, but I was looking forward to it.

'Sit yourself there, Mr Rhea,' said Annie. 'You'll have a slice then? And a mug o' tea? Milk and sugar's on t'table if you want it.'

'Thanks,' and so the feast – neither breakfast nor lunch not ten-o'clocks – got underway. She gave me a huge slice with a mountain of fresh cream as I pulled a blank crime report from my tunic pocket and placed it on the table. I put my ballpoint beside it chiefly so that I would not forget the purpose of this visit.

'I never thought there'd be all this paperwork for my old bit o' rope,' muttered Bob, as Annie placed a whopping slice of pie on his plate.

She scooped a dollop of fresh cream from a bowl and flung it on the pie, and he started to eat even before Annie had served her own share.

'Right, Bob.' I tried to regain his attention now that he was tucking into his snack. 'Full name and address of injured person. That's you. I know the answer to that. . . .'

'Injured? I've not been injured, Nick.'

'It's the term we use for the victim of a crime, Bob. Injured person, it means being the victim of a criminal. I can fill in the preliminaries because I know the answers.' I did so, but then I had to ask when the stolen property had disappeared.

'Nay, lad, you tell me. Sometime between last back-end and now. I used it when I brought my cattle indoors for t'winter so it was there then, hanging in its usual spot. And I noticed it had gone this morning.'

'And you've not given anyone permission to remove it?'

'Nay, never, it's too useful to start lending it out. You never get things back when you lend 'em to folks. It's like a workman and his tools, I need it by me all the time, just in case I have to use it.'

'Description of stolen property,' I read the heading of the section I now had to complete. 'Can you describe it, Bob?'

'Why, it's nobbut a bit of old rope, like I said.'

'I need to have some kind of description, Bob, just in case some of our other officers come across it. Length, width? Distinctive marks?'

'Well, I'd say it was about as long as a walking stick and

as thick as a sheep's front leg. And I think there's a splash o' green paint on it somewhere.'

'Hmm,' I sighed, thinking I would have to translate his estimate into feet and inches. Bob's graphic description would hardly appeal to my superiors, although the spot of green paint was an important point of identification. I therefore suggested, 'About two feet six inches long and about an inch and a half thick? And marked with a splash of green paint. Is that about right?'

'Aye,' he said. 'Summat like that.'

'So is there anything else special about your rope?'

'Aye, it's got a loop at either end, spliced into the main length.'

'A big loop?' I was still trying to gain a mental image of this rope.

'Big enough for one end to drop over t'front post of t'gate and t'other to slip over hook in the wall. You can see the hook from here.'

I looked out of the kitchen window and could see the big iron hook – I'd never noticed it before.

'So its job was to hold that gate open? I noticed it swung shut under its own weight when I came in, Bob. It needs something to hold it open at times. Luckily I was walking – I'd have had a job getting my van through if it insisted on closing itself.'

'Aye,' said Bob. 'That's exactly t'problem, Nick. You can prop it open with a stone or bit o' wood but a strong wind'll soon fettle that! Now, imagine me fetching a herd of cattle in, or flock of sheep, or even driving a car or tractor through. Yon gate would never stay open of its own accord.

You either need two folks, one to drive the animals or vehicle through and t'other to hold the gate open. Or you need summat else to hold the gate open. Anyroad, I thought two folks on those sort o' jobs was a waste of manpower. So I used that rope to hold it wide open whenever I needed it to be kept wide. I kept it handy and it saved me hours of hassle and bad tempers . . . it helped me get all my jobs done as quickly as possible.'

'Thanks, I can now see how important and useful it was. So, this is the next question on my sheet. What is its value?'

'Priceless, Nick. Absolutely priceless.'

'I can't really put that down, Bob. It would play havoc with our crime statistics. What will it cost to replace it?'

'Well, nowt, really, I've plenty of lengths of old rope or bits o' chain I could use in its place, but it's t'principal of the thing – whoever's nicked that rope has caused me a lot of extra work and worry.'

'I need a positive amount for my crime report so I'll record a nominal value of a pound,' I suggested. 'That seems about right for a piece of rope. Or maybe less? Fifteen shillings? Seventeen and six?'

'A quid is about right, Nick. Aye, we'll say that.'

'Now, finally, are you sure it's not lying around the farm somewhere? I'm supposed to make a search to be absolutely sure it has not been mislaid, but you are more capable than me of doing that.'

'I've searched high and low, Nick. Me and Annie. Not a sign of it. You can be sure o' that.'

'He's right, Mr Rhea, it's gone. We've looked everywhere.'

'So what about making an insurance claim?' was my next official question. 'Will you consider that?'

'Nay, lad, not us. I'm not one for making money out of old rope,' he chuckled. 'Do you know where that saying came from?'

'Not really.' I was now on the final corner of my slice of apple pie and was tackling the giant mug of tea as I scribbled the details on the crime report.

'In olden days,' said Bob, airing his knowledge, 'sailors would pick up all the spare bits of rope left lying around the ship. They'd sell them at the next port of call – the ropes were stripped into strands and used to fill in the gaps between the boards of decks of ships and boats; they were hammered in and then covered with tar to make the seal waterproof. And so they got money for old rope.'

'Just as you will if you make an insurance claim!' I said.

'Nay lad, I'm not that desperate.'

I don't think either Bob or Annie expected me to chase after the unknown thief or to halt passing motor vehicles to search them, but I would pass the news around the village via the pub and post office. Hopefully, someone might find it lying around the village. Nonetheless, the fact that Bob's bit of old rope had been officially reported meant it would be circulated through our Crime Informations, as the news sheets were known, and recorded in all our lists of local criminal offences. I explained all this to Bob and Annie, and they seemed satisfied with my action. I think Bob had reported the theft simply because he felt his privacy had been invaded – somebody had had the temerity to sneak into his farmyard and make off with a very useful piece of his personal property.

When I submitted my crime report to Ashfordly Sectional Office for onward transmission to sub-division, divisional office and force headquarters, I received a sharp phone call from Sergeant Bairstow.

'PC Rhea,' he said, 'are you aware of the old legal adage *De minimus non curat lex*?'

'Yes, I am, Sergeant.'

'Then why, pray, have you submitted a report about the theft of a short piece of very old rope?'

'Because it was reported to me, Sergeant, as a theft. It might not be worth much from a financial point of view, but it's priceless and most useful during the daily work of the farm in question. Its absence is causing a great deal of inconvenience.'

'But surely a farm has plenty of surplus bits of rope about the place?'

'Yes, but not this piece of rope, Sergeant.'

'If the farmer insisted on making a report, you could have exercised a little discretion by recording it as lost property!'

'I exercised my discretion by recording it as a theft, Sergeant, which is what I think it is.'

'Oh, well, if you insist. I suppose the letter of the law supports you in this but I can see we'll have another undetected crime on our books.'

'We might find the bit of rope, Sergeant.'

'Pigs might fly!' he grunted.

It would be a fortnight later when I chanced to be patrolling the area of land that included the Greengrass ranch, Hagg Bottom. The man himself was in his yard, apparently sorting out a recent delivery of scrap metal. Claude Jeremiah noticed my arrival and came to meet me. His scruffy lurcher dog, Alfred, began to sniff around my legs.

'Whatever it is, Constable Rhea, I didn't do it, I haven't got it, I've not seen it and I don't want to donate anything to police charities.'

'Have you seen a curious piece of rope in your travels?'

'Rope? How can a rope be curious?'

'It's about a yard long with a loop at either end, and a splash of green paint somewhere on it.'

In his familiar old army greatcoat, Claude Jeremiah Greengrass frowned heavily and then looked at me with a strange expression on his face. And then he began to blink heavily.

'I know we've had our differences, but we understand each other. You know I'm not a common thief.'

'Exactly, Claude. You're as honest as the day is long.'

'Well, thanks for that. If you ever leave Aidensfield, I hope your successor is as intelligent as you.'

'Which brings me back to my question – knowing you are not a thief, Claude, have you seen that odd piece of rope?'

'Because I'm not a thief and didn't steal it, I can tell you it's over there, on my wood pile.'

'And how did it get there?'

'This chap came along with a bundle of fence rails, surplus to requirements he said, and he asked if I wanted to buy them. Good timber is always valuable, Constable, so we did a deal. The bundle was held together by that piece of rope, one end looped through the other with one loop acting as a handle. He left the rope with the rails.'

'Who was he?' I asked.

'No idea,' he said, with just a hint of deviousness. 'Just an itinerant trader trying to make a bob or two. But when I saw he'd left the rope with the timber, I thought it would be very good for holding my garden gate open.'

'That's what it was used for — holding a farm gate open, and the farmer has reported it stolen.'

'Reported it? Stolen? A grotty old piece of rope like that?'

'Everything has its value, Claude.'

'You're not saying I stole it, are you? I mean, I didn't — I had no idea it wasn't his to give away . . . you'd better take it away, Constable.'

'Thanks, Claude, I will. But I think I should definitely *not* mention in my report that it was found on your premises. I'll just say it was handed to me by an anonymous person who'd heard about the theft through village gossip and he found it lying in the street. How about that? That'll stop my bosses wanting me to come and arrest you for handling stolen goods, or worse.'

'Oh, well, that's good of you, Constable. As you say, we understand each other.'

And so I took away the piece of rope, showed it to Bob and Annie who were amazed and delighted that it should turn up, and then I completed my supplementary crime report to record the recovery of the rope. I used the story I had discussed with Claude, adding that no one had been either arrested or summonsed for the crime. Indeed, there was no evidence that a crime had been committed and so, under the circumstances, I suggested the incident be written off as 'No Crime' as indeed it was. It meant, according to the records, I had not solved my most recently reported crime as the Constable of Aidensfield – but there was time for more!

And, of course, it meant I did not have an undetected crime in my current statistics.

Bob didn't have to buy himself a new piece of rope either, nor indeed any other kind of device for holding his gate open. Thanks to Claude Jeremiah Greengrass, that piece of rope and its spot of green paint continues to do its important work on the gate at Bay Tree Farm, Elsinby. Having served there for so many years, it could hardly be considered a trifle.

Chapter 4

A Call Bird Out of Bounds

Another curious incident also dwelt upon the possibility that something was far too trivial to be of concern to the police. Miss Phoebe Pettifer lived in what some would consider an idyllic situation. She owned a very charming cottage deep in Briggsby Plantation. I had never seen the house, but had been told it boasted a lot of ancient timberwork. It was very old but its history was largely unknown because all earlier records had been lost. All that was known was that the cottage had been standing on its site in 1689 and that it had been improved and modernized down the centuries. She had bought it in 1954 and, thanks to the legacy of an uncle, had been able to purchase the cottage outright and then continue to earn her living as an artist. Her subjects were odd for a sweet lady – she painted machines like classic cars, motor bikes, aircraft and ships – almost anything with an engine – and her work sold around the world either as originals or limited edition prints.

Those who knew her said she was a flamboyant lady of around sixty years of age. She had uncontrollable white hair and wore flowing, flowery dresses and skirts, coloured ribbons galore and masses of colourful beads that were almost a permanent fixture of her wardrobe. She owned an old red Ford Anglia that she used to visit the village and surrounding area – her house was at least three miles out of Briggsby and surrounded by a Forestry Commission plantation of maturing conifers. Not many people knew she lived there because the plantation was private and there were no public footpaths through it. Having never met her, I knew a surprising amount about her – that is the task of a village constable. You must get to know the people on your beat – it's called local knowledge and is invaluable in helping a constable perform his duties. Through my contacts, I got the impression she knew nothing about the natural world in which she lived. I found that odd – people who lived in such remote wooded areas were generally well informed about the wildlife around them, able to identify birds and wild flowers, butterflies and insects, trees and shrubs, but she was not interested in such things, maintaining she had bought the house simply because of the complete privacy it offered. It was something of a surprise then when Ashfordly Police Station received a phone call from her, complaining of being harassed by an unknown person.

The person, whoever it was, would knock on her door and ring the doorbell, then run away. By the time she answered the call, the visitor had vanished into the deep trees around the house.

It was Alf Ventress who called me. 'Look Nick, we don't usually get complaints from Miss Pettifer, she's not a vindictive sort of person, so this is quite unusual. The knocking noises might be the wind rocking something on the exterior of the house – a loose bit of timber somewhere, even a loose-fitting window – and the doorbell could be the result of tree branches being blown against the electricity wires which means it's really nothing to do with us. It's really a trivial matter beyond the scope of our duties, but she's a lady living alone in a remote area and it might be some local clown at work – the noises all come during the daytime, by the way.'

'In broad daylight, you mean?'

'Aye, that adds to the mystery – a determined prankster would almost certainly carry out his tricks under cover of darkness.'

'It must be frightening, hearing those noises, even in the daytime, especially if it is somebody fooling about.'

'Exactly, Nick. It's our duty to care for members of the public especially when they're victims of crime or in need of help. So I think we should help her – so can you pop in? Her house is on your patch.'

'I don't think the Forestry Commission is working in that plantation just now. So there shouldn't be anyone in the wood, either officially or unofficially, by day or by night.'

'But it sounds as if there is somebody about, Nick. Somebody with a warped mind if you ask me.'

'You could be right, Alf. I'm due for a patrol around the outskirts of Briggsby so that'll make a good task for me. I'll let you know how I get on.'

I rang Miss Pettifer to say I was coming to see her, giving an estimated time of arrival. I did so, because I did not want her to think my knocking or bell ringing was the nuisance person. Soon afterwards, I drove into the dark forest, the density of the trees being such that I thought it wise to switch on my headlights. The road was not surfaced with tarmac and although it was sound and level in places, there were some enormous potholes and signs of constant erosion of the surface. I could see where some vehicles had driven off the road to avoid ripping off their exhausts, driving along the rough verges instead.

As I drove, I passed indications of men having been at work in the forest — there were deep ruts leading into the wood, clearly caused by heavy machinery. The sides of the track were lined with stacks of cut timber, felled conifers awaiting attention and a shed or two but there was no sign of workmen.

Happily there were some primitive direction signs with one leading to Beckside Cottage. As I grew closer, I saw a small beck flowing beside the track, probably the reason for the name of the cottage. In its earlier days, out here in the middle of nowhere, I guessed it might have been a gamekeeper's lodge or a farmhand's cottage with its own fresh water supply. If Miss Pettifer hadn't taken over the hidden cottage, it would probably have become derelict, or perhaps used as a shelter for the woodmen. There were lots of derelict and abandoned stone buildings in the deeper parts of the moors.

Soon, I saw the house standing in its own clearing with a

high fence around the garden to deter foraging deer. I had never had cause to visit this lonely place and my first impression was that this was no ordinary cottage: it looked colossal, more like a manor house. Clearly, it was of very ancient origin – the rather intricate timberwork around the exterior reminded me of Tudor times; I think the house predated that era by a century or two. It was a sprawling place built of local limestone between many sturdy timber uprights and the roof was stone tiles rather than the conventional slates.

There were many windows with small panes and leaded diamonds in between, whilst different levels of that heavy stone roof suggested the house had experienced many extensions and alterations. In staring at the wonderful house in its amazingly secret location, I realized this had been no farmhand's cottage or woodman's shack. In its former days, it must have been a house of some stature and I wondered whether there had been an estate here in bygone times, this house being home to the resident lord of the manor. Had there been a takeover of one estate by another, with this house being left empty and deserted? I could find the answer by delving into local historical records, but, at the moment, I had no time for such distractions!

Rather dazzled by the house, and thinking it would be rather out of my league if I ever wanted to buy it, I parked outside the deer fence, opened the tall gate and made for the front door. Even that was remarkable. The current door appeared to be modern and had been expertly hung within the framework of a much older one. The old door frame was still in position. At each side of the modern door was a tall wooden post, probably of oak, which had been battered and weathered down the ages. Those posts disappeared into the stonework above where a stone lintel straddled the upper space, and the modern door sat comfortably inside this picturesque outer shell. The bell push was on the ancient door post to the right, neatly recessed into the surrounding timber. It reminded me of a door from an early Italian Renaissance house, or even one from Ancient Greece – it was definitely unlike any other door I'd seen in this part of England.

I found the house intriguing in many respects and wondered what it might be like to live here, but I couldn't linger in admiration and awe because Miss Pettifer would be awaiting my arrival. She'd probably noticed me driving through the trees. She had a choice of windows from which to view my arrival and, sure enough, a side door opened as I approached the front door. So I was not going to be admitted through that spectacular entry!

'Ah, PC Rhea, it's so kind of you to come. I really do appreciate it. Would like a cup of tea and a piece of cake? I really do like visitors. . . .'

She was just as I had envisaged, a larger-than-life lady in her flamboyant and colourful flowing garments and beads. She almost floated across the floor as she led me into her pretty kitchen with its window looking deep into the forest.

'Do sit down, the kettle has boiled. Milk and sugar?'

'Milk, no sugar thanks,' I said, sitting at her bare wooden table.

'I made the cakes myself, an old recipe from my

grandmother.' She placed a plateful in front of me. 'Do help yourself. . . .'

As she busied herself with brewing the tea, I tucked into one of her cakes and it was delicious. I had no idea what sort of cake it was, but it was sweet and moist with more than a hint of almonds.

She settled opposite me, poured herself a cup and smiled. Then we got down to the purpose of my visit.

'Now, PC Rhea, I know we haven't met before, but you must be wondering what all this fuss is about. An old woman being paranoid!'

'Nothing of the sort! You've reason to tell us about this. I have been told by my office in Ashfordly that you've had someone knocking on the door and ringing the bell, then disappearing.'

'Yes, it is most unsettling, Mr Rhea, and quite terrifying for a woman living on her own in this remote place. The only people who come into this wood are the forestry workers, and they have not been for a while.'

'Not even off duty? Walking dogs and such?'

'No, never. Besides, none of them would do a thing like that, they're far too decent.'

'So have you any ideas who it might be? Have you had any unannounced visitors? Met someone at one of your exhibitions, someone who might not be completely stable . . . mentally, I mean . . . a nuisance . . . a very persistent fan. . . .'

'No, no one like that. I've been racking my brains to see if I have upset anyone or had odd people wanting to talk to me . . . there's been nothing, Mr Rhea, no funny phone calls or anonymous letters. None of the usual cranky stuff. Not many people know where I live, of course.'

'Exactly, so I must ask this – have you actually seen anyone hanging around the house? Ringing your bell and running away?'

'No, no one. And the odd thing, Mr Rhea, is that the knocking and bell ringing occur during the daytime, never at night.'

'Any particular time?'

'Early morning as a rule, but sometimes in the afternoon. I have kept watch, Mr Rhea, from inside the house. I have a good view of all the approaches, but I have never seen anyone suspicious.'

'I noticed the doorbell is on that very ornate front door.'

'Yes, but I never use it. I always use the side door, the one you used.'

'So if someone rings that bell, or knocks on the front door, you respond by going to the side door?'

'I do. My studio is near the side door and I'm usually working in there; it's the easiest way of answering. And from the window of my study, I have a good view of the front door and the approaches to it. When the bell has rung, I have rushed to the window and never seen anyone. That is what is so odd about all this.'

'And it has never happened at night?'

'No, never.'

'I find that rather puzzling.' I paused a few moments to savour her tea and cakes before saying, 'There are all sorts of reasons why we hear knocks and noises around the house—'

'I know what you are going to say, PC Rhea! You're going to suggest the wind is rattling something, or it has caused the wires of the bell to misbehave . . . I've thought of that. On most occasions – and there have been more than a dozen so far – the weather has been calm and dry, with no gales or heavy rain.'

'Fair enough, but we have to examine all possibilities.' I had finished my tea and cakes, so I asked, 'Could you show me the front door please? Inside and out. And the view of it from your study window?'

'Of course.'

She led me upon a tour of her remarkable old house, including her study full of colourful paintings of cars and tractors and other machines. There was not a hint of wild life among them, not even a background tree! All her ground-floor windows, back and front, gave a wide view around the entire house, not only of its immediate surrounds, but also across the entire clearing in which her house stood and then deep into the trees. It would be almost impossible for anyone to run off without being seen. The interior of the house behind the old door was intriguing. It was an old-fashioned entrance, more of a stately reception area than the hall of a modern house.

It was very spacious and high, reaching into the roof void with a staircase and gallery at the inward side; it had a marble floor, marble pillars and bare walls decorated with murals. Our voices echoed as we chatted. From inside, I could see the modern door between the two ancient wooden pillars that looked so imposing from within the house. It was while admiring this stunning hall that I heard a rapping sound from outside. . . .

'That's it, Mr Rhea,' she whispered, her voice echoing in this vast chamber. 'Listen. . . .'

I looked around to see which of the windows offered the best view of the outside of the door and rushed across to it as she held up her finger, saying, 'Listen, it's knocking again . . . the bell will ring soon . . . just you wait and see. . . .'

I reached one of the windows, but could not see anyone and my view of the door bell was not entirely complete, but it was enough to assure me no one was standing there knocking on the door or ringing the bell. And would anyone behave like this with my police van parked prominently outside the front door?

But the knocking continued with a sharp rat-tat-tat repeated frequently, and then the bell sounded. It was a very quick ring. I waited at the window, hoping I might see the cause of this phenomenon. All I saw was a colourful bird flying off into the forest – and I had the answer.

'It's a woodpecker, Miss Pettifer,' I told her with some relief. 'A great spotted woodpecker.'

'Woodpecker, Mr Rhea?' she looked puzzled. 'Why would a woodpecker knock on my door and ring my bell? I hope it's not going to peck a hole or build a nest in my door post!'

I explained how both the male and female great spotted woodpeckers drum on resonant pieces of timber such as telegraph poles or dead trees; they deliver eight or ten powerful pecks per second so that it sounds like a miniature road drill and it is done to mark the boundaries of their territory. They also seek grubs and insects within the deep crevices of old timber where their long tongues help to locate and extract such titbits.

'I think it has been climbing up that pillar,' I said. 'Seeking grubs and when it climbs over the doorbell, which is inset and level with the woodwork, its powerful tail, which it uses for balancing on the upright wood, presses the button – and hey presto, you know you've got a visitor!'

'Are you sure, Mr Rhea? It sounds a most unlikely scenario.'

'I once knew a lady whose doorbell rang incessantly in high winds – it was an ivy twig which kept blowing against the bell push, enough to establish a contact and ring the bell.'

'I know nothing about wildlife, Mr Rhea. Maybe I should discover more of what is living and moving around me.'

'You could always paint a great spotted woodpecker on your door post,' I smiled. 'Then you could actually show the answer to incredulous visitors!'

'I have no idea what one looks like.'

'It's a highly colourful bird, chiefly black and white but with splashes of red and yellow. Very paintworthy!'

'I'll get myself a reference book of birds,' she promised herself. 'Then I'll go outside to watch it at work, I can hide somewhere, I'm sure, and maybe take a photograph. And when I paint my first woodpecker, I shall give you the painting. This might give me a whole new direction in my career – it should take my mind off clever and handsome man-made machines!'

As promised, her work arrived six months later, a nice

addition to our collection of original watercolours by local artists. She had entitled her painting 'Call Bird' which I had to look up in a reference book – it used to be a bird that was trained as a decoy, its original purpose being to entice buyers into the premises or market stall concerned. A very apt title, I thought.

Chapter 5

A Bounder to the Rescue

Thieves rarely, if ever, acknowledge the deep distress they can cause to their victims. They seem completely unaware of the harm and upset caused by their selfish behaviour. Most have no feelings of sorrow or twinges of conscience – they break into houses and steal precious goods which have taken a lifetime – or longer – to acquire. They steal purses and handbags to leave their owners penniless, often in distressing circumstances; they take cars and motor bikes and will even steal bicycles and other property from children, invalids and old people. People work for years to afford their precious belongings yet thieves remove them without any compassion.

They steal from shops and supermarkets, somehow thinking the goods on display are fair game, and some will remove full charity donation tins from the bars of inns and other public places. They will even raid churches to rifle offertory boxes or collection plates placed there for charitable donations. In other words thieves have no shame, no conscience and no sense of sinfulness. Psychological theories that thieves are themselves deprived people in need of our help and succour are widely seen as absolute rubbish. In simple terms, they steal because they are greedy, selfish and obnoxious.

Any police officer, retired or still serving, can relate tales of deep distress caused by thieves. One must wonder whether a thief, confronted with the distress he or she has created, can ever feel compassion or grief.

It was during my routine patrols of Aidensfield that I became aware of the actions of a thief or thieves whose appalling and greedy behaviour caused immense stress to two innocent families. It all began when a pleasant house in Aidensfield was known to be coming on the market; houses and cottages in the village were always in demand. Known as Buttercup Cottage, it was on the main street, not far from the post office, and was a detached stone-built property set in a small area of garden. It had five good bedrooms, plenty of accommodation downstairs, a good spacious and light kitchen, several outbuildings to the rear including an outdoor toilet. It also boasted a fairly modern bathroom with an indoor toilet upstairs. It had a stone-built garage which was large enough to accommodate a family car and several cycles. However, it had been empty for several years and its neglect was beginning to show in peeling paint, cracked windows, one or two loose tiles and the mass of ivy that covered its walls and roof. I did not know whether it had a damp course but guessed its interior would have suffered, having stood empty for something like ten or twelve years. In spite of its neglected appearance, though, the structure was sound and the roof was weather-proof.

I do not know how the rumour started that it was coming onto the market, but I heard it in the village shop. It was Jack Carver, the shopkeeper, who mentioned it. 'If you know anybody who wants a good house in this vicinity, Nick, they could do worse than get hold of Buttercup Cottage.'

'But it's been empty for years, Jack. It'll need a lot of work and expense to put it right – I doubt if it's habitable in its present state. Not many folks can afford to spend a lot once they've bought a property.'

'It's as solid as a rock, Nick, and as dry as a bone. And it has been modernized up to a point. They knew how to build houses in those days. I've got a key for it – the owners live near Manchester and can't get over here to maintain it as often as they would like. So, if you hear of anyone who's interested, let me know.'

'So it's just been left to God and providence?' I smiled.

'Some members of the family, long before the war, bought it as a second home, a holiday cottage to be enjoyed by all members of the family, but, as time went by, the up-and-coming younger generations couldn't be bothered with it. I don't think they had enough money to enjoy it or keep it in good order. They didn't even rent it out as a holiday cottage – it would require a lot of work and expense to make it fit for that.'

'So what makes you think it might be coming up for sale?' I asked.

'I got a call from the estate agent who looks after it; he rang to ask if I still had a key because someone in the vicinity was expressing interest and might wish to look around the house with a view to making an offer.'

'So who's that?'

'Search me.' He shrugged his shoulders. 'They wouldn't tell me, but I assured them I still kept the key in a secure place. They said they would contact me if there was any development.'

'So, is it being advertised on the open market, or is this deal being done privately?'

'I think it's a private arrangement, Nick. Someone has made an unexpected offer and the owners are considering it. That's all I know.'

'I won't be making an offer; village bobbies can't buy houses unless they move away to a new posting' I said. 'And even then it's not easy, the force doesn't fall over itself to give police officers permission to buy their own houses. Besides, if I ever needed to buy a place, I'd need one I could walk into without having to do much repair work. A shortage of funds and the expense of a big family wouldn't allow me to modernize a place like Buttercup Cottage, attractive though it is. So you can count me out.'

'I understand, Nick. But I thought you should be aware that it's likely to come onto the market. It might mean strangers coming to live here.'

'It would be better being used than being allowed to

deteriorate – apart from anything else, it might become unsightly.'

I left him and then took a long and more critical look at the old cottage as I walked past. I felt sure the necessary modifications would be beyond do-it-yourself abilities – it would require professional craftsmen to make a decent job of any modernization scheme. Even something basic like checking the electrical and plumbing systems would require professional expertise. As I was scheduled to undertake a foot patrol of Aidensfield that day, which included most of the farms around the outskirts, I took one last look at Buttercup Cottage, then made my way to Moorside Farm on the hill behind Aidensfield. It was a large and successful mixed arable, sheep and dairy farm owned by Les and Marjory Marshall. Their daughter, Susan, was getting married in about three weeks time and I wanted to know as much detail as possible about the required parking arrangements around the church. I would make a point of being on duty at the time of the wedding, hopefully to ensure the bride and her guests got to the church with the minimum of trouble and that matters like the photographs were completed satisfactorily without causing a traffic jam in Aidensfield. If necessary, I would arrange for parking cones to be placed on all approaches to the church to prevent indiscriminate parking.

This was one example of many unofficial duties performed by local constables, but a small thoughtful action of this kind always paid dividends so far as the police image and reputation was concerned. It was midmorning when I arrived, my route being the long drive up through the fields to the farmhouse via an iron bridge that rattled as I drove across it. The bridge, crossing a deep, fast-flowing stream that ran between two of the larger fields, also served as a cattle grid so that no gate was needed at that location.

With widely-spaced round iron bars forming its surface, the bridge was broad enough to permit the passage of the largest tractor or combine harvester, but no cow or sheep could walk across it. Their cloven hoofs would simply slip into the hollow beneath – they'd learned about those risks very quickly! Cattle grids are a feature of many moorland roads and are a simple method of containing sheep within their strays whilst not inconveniencing motorists with frequent stops to open and shut gates.

When I arrived, I was invited into the kitchen to enjoy a mug of coffee and to share a massive fruitcake. I explained my suggestions to Mr and Mrs Marshall and they gave details of the timings of the wedding – a three o'clock service lasting about forty-five minutes, followed by the reception on the farm premises. I obtained the figures for family members and the numbers of official guests, in all amounting to almost 200. A big wedding by any standards. I said I would cone off the church at noon before the wedding and the cones would remain *in situ* until half an hour after the wedding photos had been taken outside the church. The reception would be in a marquee at the farm and the wedding party would drive from the church in both official and private cars, but I had no concerns about parking there. It was on private property with plenty of room on level fields and was not my concern; I was assured those parking arrangements would be overseen by the ushers and other family members. There was ample space and the surface of every field to be used was sound enough to accommodate most types of motor vehicle.

It was during this visit I discovered the Marshalls had put in an offer for Buttercup Cottage, the idea being to renovate it for Susan. Meanwhile, she and her new husband would live in a farmhand's cottage within the farm's complex. I knew the Marshalls had the money and capability to improve Buttercup Cottage beyond recognition. Undoubtedly, it would make a nice home for Susan and her new husband.

I returned to my police house to make a formal request for the sergeant at Ashfordly to officially order the traffic cones and asking that this larger-than-normal wedding be included in the section diary. That note would ensure good police coverage even if I was unable to attend for any reason – after all, something more drastic might occur. Real police work had to take priority over the courtesy of policing social events.

On the morning of the wedding, a Saturday, I was up at seven o'clock, preparing to receive a trailerload of cones from traffic division, and to check that all our plans were being fulfilled. Then, shortly before 7.30 I got a very agitated telephone call from Les Marshall, father of the bride.

'Nick,' he said. 'You've got to come quickly. Now in fact.'

'What's the matter, Les?' His voice told me something

was seriously wrong.

'Somebody's stolen that iron bridge of mine – the lot. It's gone . . . lock, stock and barrel. Overnight.'

'The entire bridge?' I was aghast at the news.

'Aye, the lot. We can't get out of the farm now, we can't cross the beck and it's the wedding today with lots to do before the service . . . and all the guests are coming to the marquee this afternoon. The caterers and hairdresser need to be in early too. God, this is awful, Nick, a right disaster. Can you find my bridge? It can't have gone far, it was there last night. Alert all your colleagues, the radio stations, newspapers . . . we must have it back. We're marooned without it.'

'But how could anyone steal an entire bridge?' I asked.

'They'd need heavy lifting gear, Nick, say a mobile crane. And the bridge was rigid enough – and small enough – to be lifted away in its entirety – it wouldn't need to be dismantled, but it would need a low-loader to cart it away. Obviously someone needs a bridge, or else it will be broken up and sold for scrap. You can get £7.10s.0d. or more per ton for scrap metal and that bridge must weigh ten tons or so. It's unbelievable anyone would do this to us.'

'I'll have to come and visit the scene,' I said. 'I need a detailed description and any identifying marks on the metal struts.'

'But you can't get across the beck, Nick, we'd have to shout across the water and besides, every minute you're talking to me, the thieves will be getting further away . . . you've got to find them and stop them.'

'I can't get my colleagues to look for a low loader carrying a stolen bridge if I don't have some kind of description, Les. Look, I'll issue a general All-Stations Warning before I leave home, just in case some of our patrols, or those further afield, notice a bridge of any kind being carried on the roads. We can always conduct checks in such cases, but from you I'll need a detailed description.'

'Aye, right, I'll see you at the site in ten minutes.'

Through sub-divisional headquarters at Eltering, I arranged for an urgent All-Stations radio message to be transmitted throughout the North of England and further afield, briefly describing the circumstances, but saying that a detailed description of the stolen property was not yet available. I hoped some alert officer would notice such a load being carried on one of our roads but without knowing when it departed from our locality, it was difficult to know how far it might have travelled. Clearly, a major theft of this kind is never undertaken without very careful advance planning and, privately, I worried that we might never find it. It would be beyond the range of the local police long before it had been reported missing.

At this very moment, it might be installed somewhere, perhaps after being hastily repainted as a disguise, or it might be hidden in a warehouse ready to be demolished and re-erected elsewhere, or already it might even have been cut up for scrap – and all before we were made aware that it was missing. But, I told myself, you'd think an iron bridge would be easy to spot on our roads, even if it was hundreds of miles away?

When I arrived at the gap where the bridge had been, Les Marshall was already waiting at the other side of the beck.

Fortunately, there was no wind and the water, some three feet deep, was flowing gently between the high banks and so we could shout to one another. Although it was hardly the best means of conducting an interview for a crime report, it would have to suffice for the time being.

'Time's ticking away, Nick, we've caterers coming soon, and the hairdresser, my wife and daughter . . . and we must get across that beck to get to the church.'

'Isn't there another way?' I asked, perhaps naïvely. I knew that the fields of some moorland farms were linked by gates where ancient green tracks had once been the main thoroughfares. 'Through a neighbouring farm?'

'Not without knocking a few walls down, Nick, or taking up a hedge or two, and that's not as easy as you might think, especially with my neighbour. We're not exactly on speaking terms – he blamed a hole in one of my fences for my sheep eating all his new sugar beet tops. Besides taking a wall down or uprooting a hedge isn't done in a few minutes.'

'I understand the difficulties, Les, but under these circumstances, might he take a different view?'

'He might, if he was here. They're away, him and his missus, they've left one of their men in charge till next weekend.'

'And he won't feel like making such a big decision?'

'Nay, he won't but I suppose I could bash my way through a wall without telling him, so I can get onto his land and use his driveway, and then I'd tell him what I've done . . . that often works best. Desperate problems need desperate actions. But if I did that, he might retaliate by blocking his drive with the combine or summat. This needs careful thought, Nick, and I've a bit of time left before I do summat daft . . . not much, but enough to get me calmed down. There must be an answer somewhere.'

'Right, Les, I'll leave that problem with you, but meanwhile I've circulated a brief description of the bridge; every police station, patrol car and patrolling bobby in the country will be aware of it, but I still need a more detailed description, just to be sure that if we do find a bridge on the move, it really is yours.'

'Aye, right, I understand.'

He told me it was built of iron painted a dark green and comprised a series of box girders and struts bolted together to form the bridge. It was some twenty-two feet long by fifteen feet wide, with the base comprising round metal bars with gaps between – i.e. in the form of a cattle grid. It had low parapets, each being about a yard high with a broad top and a criss-cross vertical pattern running along their length. He also remembered it bore an oval brass plate bearing the manufacturer's name – BRADSHAW OF THORNABY-ON-TEES. That was bolted to one of the lower exterior girders – probably the first thing to be removed by the thieves.

The entire bridge had been in position last night at 10 p.m. and he noticed it missing this morning shortly before 7 a.m. That was nine hours – and even a vehicle with such a heavy load could travel a long way before the alarm was raised, allowing for the time taken to remove the bridge.

Having seen the bridge on those occasions when I had visited the farm, I now had sufficient information to consolidate my earlier report and did so by radio from my parked van. It was difficult producing a value – for serving the farm, the bridge was priceless; even if it was worth £750 as scrap metal, it might only bring £150-£200 as stolen property.

Having given me these details, I could see Les was anxious to return to his family to try and find some means of crossing the beck or else bulldozing a route through his neighbour's property, so I left him to his problems. I would begin my own enquiries by asking local farmers and people living nearby whether they had heard or seen anything untoward during the night hours. The snag with seeing a low-loader driving away with a bridge on board is not, in itself, suspicious; who would dream such a thing had been stolen? But the sight of a bridge on the move might excite some interest. I hoped it had!

As it was not yet eight o'clock, the Marshalls still had some time – albeit very little – on their side but even if my colleagues found the bridge, it was doubtful if it could be replaced in time for the wedding. Despite the relatively early hour, I parked in Aidensfield and began to quiz people who were already on the move around the village.

The shop was open, for example, with people popping in for morning papers and breakfast items and so the main street was surprisingly busy. And then I saw Claude Jeremiah Greengrass, with his dog Alfred at his heel, heading towards the shop.

'Just the fellow!' I hailed him.

'What have I done now, Constable?' He grinned cheekily. 'It must be summat serious to get you out of bed this early.'

'I don't think this one's down to you, Claude; I reckon it's a bit out of your league. Les Marshall's had his iron bridge stolen – sometime during the night or early this morning.'

Claude didn't reply for a few minutes, wrinkling up his face and blinking his eyes in what was clearly a combination of amazement and incredulity. 'That iron bridge across his beck? You're joking!'

'I'm not, Claude; it was spirited away during the night.'

'Not washed away by a flood then? Or collapsed with rust or summat?'

'No, Claude. Stolen. Vanished. The whole thing. As clean as a whistle. The Marshalls are marooned in their farm right now.'

'Well, blow me. I've never come across that before. I've known thieves nick some strange and weighty items, but never a whole bridge. I once knew some villains who stole six miles of railway lines and another who nicked a ten-foot high statue of Venus from a stately home's garden. But a bridge?'

'Well, it's happened right here in Aidensfield, Claude. So did you hear or see anything during the night?'

'Not a thing, Constable. Slept like a log, I did. But I am amazed . . . I must admit I don't know anybody round here who could spirit away a bridge as if it was nothing more than a gnome in the garden.'

'Well, keep your ears and eyes open, Claude. I'd appreciate a call if you do remember anything, or have any idea who might be behind this.'

'Aye, well, it would be nice if you could recover it because isn't that lass of Marshall's supposed to be getting wed today?'

'She is, that's one of the problems that's been caused. We don't know how she's going to get to the church.'

'Well, if I were you, Constable, and if you want to create a good impression in the village, you should have words with Major Kenneth Owen at Catterick Camp. Right now.'

'And who might he be?'

'I don't know the name of his unit, but when my old mate Harry Newton had his bridge washed away in floods a few years ago, Major Owen's lot came out and installed a Bailey bridge or was it a pontoon? Anyway, it cost Harry nowt − the army called it an emergency exercise and regarded it as a training scheme. It wasn't permanent − just a temporary bridge to keep his vehicles moving until he could arrange a permanent new one. And it was done in less than a day.'

'Really?'

'Aye, well, he said the army often has to cross rivers and ravines at short notice in wartime conditions, so they've all kinds of bridges they can build quickly as temporary measures. They're very expert at installing temporary bridges at short notice. The trouble is they need regular practice in real emergency conditions to keep their bridge-building skills highly tuned, and that kind of practice is hard to come by. Assault bridges, trestle bridges, pontoons,

Bailey bridges – you name it, the army can fix one in a twinkling of an eye. They have to, lives might depend on it.'

'Thanks, Claude, you might have saved the day! I'll go straight home and ring Major Owen.'

When eventually I contacted the Catterick Camp switchboard, I was told that there was no Major Owen among the personnel. Rather disappointed, I explained my purpose and was told, 'Oh, you need his successor, Major Swann – nobody can build a Bailey bridge faster than Major Swann and his team, PC Rhea. I'll put you through.'

When Swann answered in his crisp Sandhurst accent, I explained the Marshalls' dilemma with details of the timing of the wedding, and he said, 'PC Rhea, this is just the sort of challenge I need for my men. A real emergency situation where a temporary bridge is called for. But we have to move fast so where do I find Mr Marshall?'

I provided the Marshalls' telephone number, address and a map reference for his farm, then Swann said, 'Leave it with us, Mr Rhea. There will be a bridge across that beck in time for the wedding. Guaranteed! Nobody has yet beaten Swann in a bridge-building challenge!'

'That's wonderful news!' I wasn't quite sure how to thank him.

'Wonderful for us too, Mr Rhea. Do you mind if I contact KAPE?'

'KAPE?' I puzzled.

'Our public relations office. That's their slogan – KAPE. Keep the Army in the Public Eye. This would be a wonderful piece of publicity for us, a good human interest story – the army getting the bride to the church on time.'

'I see no problem about publicity, but have a word with Mr Marshall, just to be on the safe side.'

'I will, thanks, old chap.'

I waited at home for a few minutes, wondering if the Major would confirm he would be attending, but within a few minutes it was Les who rang.

'Nick,' he said, in a voice that was almost tearful 'I've just had the army on the line . . . they're going to install a Bailey bridge in time for the wedding . . . they said you'd contacted them!'

'Actually, it was a tip I'd got from Claude Jeremiah Greengrass, so let's hope it works.'

'Well, the chap who rang me said he'd never failed yet. Look, maybe you and your wife would like to join us at the reception? A small way of saying thank you. And Claude of course. And the army team . . . we must include them.'

'We'd love to Les, so thanks for the thought. I'll be there if the bridge is installed in time!'

'So will all of us!' he said.

And the shaky, rattling Bailey bridge was installed and safely put into use by 2.30. It meant some of the pre-wedding tasks were slightly delayed, but it enabled the bride to get to the church on time. The guests enjoyed a wonderful reception in the marquee too. During the speeches, the groom and his extended new family went to great lengths to thank Claude as well as the wonderful heroism and skills of the bridge builders who had been allowed by their commanding officer to attend the reception. It was a most happy occasion and, thanks to KAPE, the story got into the local papers with headlines like: ARMY BRIDGE GETS BRIDE TO THE CHURCH ON TIME or SWANN AROUND TO GET BRIDE TO CHURCH ON TIME.

Two days later, the stolen bridge, now a different colour, was found otherwise unharmed in a warehouse in the suburbs of Manchester. Two men were arrested and eventually the bridge was returned to its rightful place, its only other damage being the missing maker's plate.

Chapter 6

Bound By Red Tape

If it seems strange that thieves would steal an entire bridge, then it might be possible to believe they could remove an entire building by stealth, not something like a garden shed or greenhouse, but a structure that was rather more substantial.

One Sunday afternoon I was on duty in Ashfordly, performing cover duties because all the Ashfordly bobbies were either on leave, away on a course or working a late shift. I was covering the four hours between 2 p.m. and 6 p.m. when the town was busy with tourists; the only shops open were touristy places such as the pubs, small cafés and souvenir shops, although the castle ruins were open to visitors. The more conventional shops like the greengrocer, butcher, grocer, newsagent, chemist and so on were all closed. At weekends and bank holidays, Ashfordly is over-run by masses of tourists, so the residents keep away or get their revenge by becoming tourists in some other place.

I was standing in front of the Lord Ashfordly Memorial in the market-place when a middle-aged, balding man approached me.

He was dressed casually and my first thought was that he was a tourist seeking advice or directions.

'Excuse me, Constable, but can I have a word?' Now that he was close to me I could see the worried frown on his face.

'Of course.' I tried a friendly smile. 'How can I help?'

'I hope you don't think I'm stupid, but somebody has stolen my warehouse.'

'Warehouse?' I cried. 'An entire warehouse?'

'Yes, that's why I can't really believe what has happened. I've been pinching myself to show I'm not dreaming.'

'Well, we had someone steal a complete iron bridge recently, but I'd say a warehouse was a different matter. What was it built of?'

'Timber and asbestos sheets,' he said. 'With an asbestos sheet roof. Cement floor. Locking double doors at the front, two windows along each side. It was about the size of a double garage, maybe just a shade longer.'

'Not bricks and mortar then?'

'No, so I suppose it would be easily portable.'

'So where was it?' was my next question.

'Just off Station Road,' he said. 'There is a patch of council land down there, the new small business park, and I rented space for my warehouse. I've been using it for years – although it has been standing empty recently. There was nothing in it when it was stolen.'

'So when did it go missing?'

'Sometime between last March and today.'

'So it could have been missing for ten or twelve weeks?'

'No, longer than that; more than a year, Constable. March last year, I mean. Not this year. I live in Leeds, you see, and only get across here once in a while. Because it was empty, I didn't bother to come, but now I've won a big contract for supplying bathroom furnishings and fittings, I thought I would store some of them in my Ashfordly warehouse. I came over today for a recce – and discovered it had vanished.'

'We'd better go and have a look,' I said. 'So, meanwhile, what's your name?'

'Morris, Patrick Morris.'

At a brisk pace, he led me from the market square, down Bridge Street and along Riverside Road until we reached the council-owned land which was being developed as a small industrial estate. He led me through a labyrinth of alleys and roads until we reached a patch of ground knee deep in grass, nettles and weeds. In the middle of the undergrowth I could see a cement base which reminded me of the huts used formerly by prisoners-of-war or refugees. The base was about eight yards long by six yards wide and at what I guessed had been the entrance, there was a small tarmac surfaced drive.

'It was right here,' he stated, standing in the centre of the base. 'Now it's gone. Not a piece left . . . if it had been destroyed in a gale, there'd be some remains, but, look. Nothing. Absolutely nothing.'

'Could it be easily dismantled?' I asked.

'Yes, I would say so. Any competent person could demolish it by undoing a few nuts and bolts, and having a trailer or wagon to put it into.'

'And a value, Mr Morris? For my crime report?'

'Not a lot, it cost me six hundred pounds to buy and erect seven or eight years ago. Cheap really, but I couldn't afford a stone-built or brick warehouse.'

'If it's been dismantled by thieves, it will be difficult to identify as yours. It could be reassembled in a different form,' I had to warn him. 'Were there any identifying marks on it? Your company name perhaps?'

'There was a wooden sign near the entrance saying *Patrick Morris Merchandising* and the address – Unit 17, Station Road Business Park, Ashfordly with my Leeds phone number. But that was all. They'd soon get rid of that.'

I wrote down all his personal details and a description of the missing warehouse, promising him I would circulate details through normal police channels. In view of the lengthy time lapse since he had last seen it, I expressed my doubts that it would be recovered but said I would immediately commence enquiries in Ashfordly and district in the hope I produced some clue as to its whereabouts.

He was a reasonable man who appreciated the difficulties, and I said I would contact him the moment I had any further news. He said he was returning to Leeds within the next hour and thanked me for my attention.

Station Road Business Park had grown surprisingly quickly once the council realized the potential of letting sites to small, expanding enterprises and currently it was home to a variety of outlets, ranging from a ladies' fashion house to motor vehicle body shop. There would be about thirty warehouses and offices of various sizes, and recently the council had laid down some surfaced access roads to cater for further growth. As Mr Morris made his way home, I began my enquiries on the site but, being a Sunday, most of the offices and warehouses were closed. I failed to find anyone who had noticed the warehouse being demolished, nor did I find anyone who had noticed any unusual activity around it. Similarly my enquiries in the town, especially in streets close to the industrial site, failed to reveal any useful information. I decided to resume my enquiries on Monday when the business park would be open and in the meantime would enter details in the crime register at Ashfordly Police Station. From that, details of the theft would be circulated throughout the county. There was little else I could do at this stage.

On the Monday morning, however, I was scheduled for a 9 a.m.-5 p.m. tour of duty and so, with the sergeant's approval, decided to spend as much time as necessary in Ashfordly making enquiries about the missing warehouse. My first efforts had to be the industrial estate, now with offices and warehouses fully staffed, and so I thought I might learn something.

And I did.

'There were some men working there a few weeks ago,' said Jim Proud who ran a small stationery suppliers and office furnishing business on the site. 'I saw them taking the warehouse to pieces. They had a lorry with them. I never thought they were thieves . . . well, you don't, do you? Bold as brass, they were. Working in broad daylight.'

'Could you describe them? Number of men? Ages? Dress? Details of their lorry?'

'There were three of them, I remember that, but I can't describe them. They looked like council workmen to me, overalls and such, middle-aged chaps, well, in their forties mebbe. They got here at half-eight one morning with their lorry and worked through till half-four that afternoon.'

'And no one questioned their presence?'

'No, a lot of us noticed what was going on, but we thought it was the council demolishing the old warehouse. It had been empty for ages. They pulled it down and got it away in one day.'

'Can you recall anything about the lorry? Did it have any markings or name on it?'

'To be honest, I never noticed. It was just an ordinary lorry – dark-green colour, I think – being loaded up with the remains of the warehouse.'

I recalled Patrick Morris saying his warehouse was worth only £600, hardly worth the efforts of a team of thieves working a full day – if they tried to sell it, they would only realize a fraction of that amount. Now, though, I had a good line of enquiry – I needed to know if the supposed council workmen were genuine. It was time to visit Ashfordly Rural District Council offices. It took a while for me to find the right person in the right department – councils worked in strange ways, highly compartmentalized with one office not really knowing what another was doing.

I was passed between public health, street collections, finance including rating and valuation, engineering and surveying, the clerk's department and chief executive's office before I found someone who might help. He was a Mr Charles Gladwin and he worked in the department dealing with the new industrial site. It was a one-man department called forward planning.

'So, PC Rhea, how can I help?'

I explained I was anxious to determine whether a team of council workmen had recently demolished unit 17 on the industrial park, as I had received an allegation of theft of the building. I stressed I was not accusing the council of theft, but merely checking the truth of the story.

'Ah,' he said. 'That could be engineering and surveying. I'll call them, to save you traipsing around the corridors.'

'I've already been there,' I said.

'Ah, yes, but perhaps you did not ask the right question of the right person. One second.'

He dialled on his intercom and said, 'Miss Jackson? Can you spare a minute please. It's Gladwin from forward planning. Can you bring the files on the industrial estate, unit 17 in particular, leased by a man called Patrick Morris.'

She must have given a positive response, because he said, 'She'll be here in a couple of minutes. Now, a coffee perhaps?' He rang for three coffees and, as they arrived, so did Miss Jackson. She was a tall and very slender woman in her early fifties, with heavy dark-rimmed spectacles and a hairstyle that looked like a throw-back to World War II. She wore a grey cardigan over a white blouse; her skirt was also grey and she was clutching a thick blue file. I would bet she had worked here all her life, probably since being a teenager.

'Ah, Miss Jackson, take a seat. There is coffee. Now, this is PC Rhea from Aidensfield. He will explain.'

I began. 'I'm investigating the report of an unusual theft, Miss Jackson. Mr Patrick Morris has reported the theft of his warehouse. It occupied unit 17 on the industrial estate. I have made enquiries from the owners of neighbouring units and it appears that some time ago they saw what appeared to be a team of council workmen demolishing the warehouse and carrying it away in a lorry. I am not accusing the council of theft, but I am anxious to establish the truth of that sighting.'

'Ah,' she said, 'Just a moment.' And she opened her file and began to flick through the contents. I waited and so did Mr Gladwin. Eventually she said, 'Ah, yes, we have a note that unit 17 no longer exists – the site is ripe for further development, which is my department, but to establish the reason for its disappearance, you need to speak to rating and valuation, that's part of finance. I suggest Mr Prothero. Shall I ask him to come here?'

'Yes, please, Miss Jackson,' said Mr Gladwin.

Ten minutes later a small, balding and rather plump, bespectacled man of 45 years of age or thereabouts, arrived with a file under his arm, and was invited to sit down and take coffee. Once again, I repeated the story. Mr Prothero listened in silence.

'Ah yes, PC Rhea, the story is quite true. The council authorized demolition of unit 17 in June last year. It was demolished later, after allowing time for an appeal from the tenant.'

'But the owner, or tenant, or whatever he is, thinks it has been stolen,' I stressed. 'Clearly he knew nothing about this until he arrived yesterday.'

'Hmm,' said Mr Prothero. 'We have a thick file of correspondence about unit 17. We wrote to the owner many times, but none of our letters was answered and we concluded Mr Morris had either gone away or died.'

'Can I ask why you wrote to him?'

'As you know, Mr Rhea, council rates and rentals invariably rise at each new financial year. We wrote to Mr Morris before the end of the last financial year, explaining the increase in rates and rental for unit 17, but we also included a letter to say the council was anxious to improve the visual image of the industrial site. We had noted unit 17 was very shabby and neglected and proposed that it be demolished – appropriate compensation would be paid. Our letters stated categorically that unless we heard from Mr Morris within three months, our proposals would go ahead. We received no acknowledgement or communication from him, certainly not within the time scale allowed, and so the demolition took place. That was last September – we've heard nothing from him since that time and we proposee to construct a new brick-built office on the site, and let it to suitable tenants.'

'But he told me he knew nothing of this. . . .'

'I can assure you he did know, Mr Rhea. Look, here is a copy of the final letter we sent. Indeed, when our workmen got inside the warehouse, they found a pile of mail, including letters from the council, all of which were unopened.'

'You sent the letters to the warehouse?' I asked.

'Of course, that is his business address.'

'But he lives in Leeds,' I told them. 'And his telephone number was on a board outside the warehouse. Surely someone rang him, or got in touch with his Leeds address before going ahead with the demolition order. Couldn't you have checked whether he was paying his rates, and rent too?'

There was a long and telling silence, a good indication to me that the right hand of the council had no idea what the left hand was doing. Even at this early stage, it was clear someone had made a glorious pig's-ear of this. I felt sorry for Patrick Morris, caught up as he was inside a typical bureaucratic example of red tape strangling enterprise.

'If that warehouse was demolished illegally,' I said quietly, 'The council could find themselves charged with malicious damage, or even theft of the component parts.'

Mr Prothero got to his feet. 'I will check it immediately, PC Rhea, and I am pleased you have brought this to our notice. Rest assured that if the council has made a mistake, I will contact Mr Morris personally, by telephone.'

'I'll call again on Thursday to see what progress you have made.' I wondered if my words sounded like a veiled threat, which they were.

'Yes, I fully understand you need to finalize your files, Mr Rhea.'

And so I left the council offices as the three officials went into a huddle. Before booking off duty, I rang Mr Morris at Leeds to explain the progress I had made.

'Thanks, Mr Rhea,' he said. 'I've already had a very

apologetic man ring me from Ashfordly Council. Not one of his letters has come to me at this address, they all went to unit 17 and never got answered, yet my payments for rent and rates are up to date, paid through bankers' orders. Clearly, there's a lack of communication between council departments.'

'Same old story – red tape! It happens at local council level, county council level and government level,' I commiserated with him.

'Well, some good's come out of all this. They have plans to build a small brick office on the site but they say the architect's department at County Hall can easily convert it into a warehouse, complete with electrical circuits and hot and cold running water! It'll even have a toilet – now there's a luxury! As a form of apology, I've been offered the new warehouse at the rates I paid for the old shack . . . wonderful stuff, Mr Rhea, even if it will take another six months for the new place to be built. They have found me an old warehouse in the meantime, so I can go ahead with my plans . . . so all's well that ends well.'

Mr Morris insisted on giving a donation to police charities and I suggested our Widows and Orphans Fund; he said he would send a cheque but I did not ask the amount.

But I did make a mental note to visit his new warehouse if ever I should buy a new home – after all, I might need my bathroom and toilet upgrading and he would be just the fellow to make sure I got a good deal.

There is one final story about thieves that I enjoyed. A block of flats in an inner city area was constantly raided by burglars and thieves with valuables of every kind being stolen. The residents had lost almost all their precious belongings and so they decided to erect a large notice outside to warn the thieves that any further raids would be futile.

It said:

Notice to Thieves.
Others have been here before you. All cameras, binoculars, music systems, transistor radios, television sets, diamond rings, pearls, necklaces, watches, antiques, pictures and crockery have been stolen. Even worthless jewellery and paperback books have been taken. There is nothing left on these premises that is worth stealing.

There was. It was that sign. Someone stole it.

Chapter 7

Bound to Be Guilty

Among the most terrible of personal disasters is when someone is falsely accused of committing a crime. Much worse, of course, is when an innocent person is tried and found guilty by the courts, particularly if that crime carries a sentence of imprisonment or some deep social stigma. In the past, murder carried the death penalty in this country with the last judicial hangings occurring on 13 August, 1964 (two on that same day) and unfortunately there have been instances where innocent people have been executed. It is almost impossible to imagine the torment in the minds of such victims and their loved ones – our legal system, said to be the finest in the world with all its benefits and safeguards, is not free from error, and never has been.

It is despicable therefore that there are those who

deliberately set out to frame an innocent person so that the courts reach a finding of guilt in spite of denials by the accused. And, it has to be said, there are those who are easily convinced of the guilt of a person even when that person is completely innocent. If a witness provides unchallenged evidence to the police, or before a court of law, it is difficult for a genuine and honest verdict to be reached. Even in our courts, innocent people are vulnerable to the machinations of accomplished liars.

To falsely accuse a person of a crime is the action of the worst of our nation's low-life, but when I was serving as a policeman, my colleagues and I were constantly aware that we could be framed. It was quite within the bounds of possibility that we might be accused of an offence we had not committed. That form of revenge was often used by the worst of the criminal classes; the purpose was quite simply to get a copper – any copper – sacked and to have him or her fitted up with a criminal record and a ruined career. The fact that the innocent officer's career was destroyed and his family left devastated and often homeless was never considered. In that way, it meant members of his or her family were also punished by the false accusation.

One of the simplest ways was to accuse a police officer of theft with the allegation being supported by irrefutable evidence. This was achieved by one of the conspirators walking into a police station on the pretence of finding a wallet, purse or handbag.

In legitimate circumstances, the object in question would be handed over to the police. The duty officer would make a record of the finding in the Found Property register, including details such as the date, time and place of the finding, along with the name and address of the finder. Most important, however, was for the police officer to check the contents in the presence of the finder – most wallets, purses or handbags contained money and other valuables. To check the contents in the presence of the finder prevented the police officer from being later accused of theft if the finder claimed cash or valuables had disappeared since the time he or she had last been in possession of the property. It sometimes happened that when lost property was found, the first finder would rifle it for money, valuables or jewellery, and then throw it away. Along would come a second honest finder who would take possession of it and report the finding to the police. By doing so, he or she would promptly be under suspicion of stealing the missing contents.

To make use of found property as a means of framing a police officer for theft, therefore, the conspirator would dash into the police station and plonk the 'found' handbag, wallet or purse on the counter, but before being asked to give his name and address, he would dash out, saying he had a bus or train to catch. In that way, he preserved his anonymity. I say 'he' but of course, it could be a woman. The police officer was then left with a valuable item of property, the precise contents of which had not been checked. In fact, it would not contain any money.

If that police officer was experienced or sensible, he would summon a colleague to immediately assist him to check its contents – but in a busy police station, such assistance was not always immediately available.

What happened next was that, sometime later (certainly after the police had changed shifts or even the following day), the second conspirator would walk into the same police station to report losing the property in question. From the detailed description provided, the property found earlier could be regarded as theirs, but before signing for it, they would be asked to check the contents. That's when the loser claimed all the money had gone – it was usually a sensible figure and not something outrageous: maybe twenty or thirty pounds in notes with a few shillings and pence in cash, more than enough to get a police officer convicted and sacked.

The missing cash immediately suggested a crime had been committed with two suspects in the frame, i.e. the finder, or the police officer who dealt with the initial report. The officer currently dealing with the matter was not the one who had earlier accepted the found property – so he was not under suspicion. However, this allegation meant that his colleague who had first dealt with the found property was under grave suspicion and it would be the current officer's duty to report the matter to a senior officer. The property in question would be retained until the matter had been finalized – and so a crime enquiry would be launched.

During the next day or so, the original 'finder' would walk into the police station, saying he was back in the area for a while and thought he would check on the found property he had brought in earlier. He would explain he was sorry he'd had to dash off without leaving his details but was now happy to provide them. When it was discovered the property was now the subject of a crime enquiry, he would be interviewed, first as a suspected thief and then as a witness. He would falsely claim that when he had handed the property to the police officer on the desk, it contained two pound notes along with some silver and copper. In this way, therefore, the innocent police officer who had been staffing the counter would find himself or herself the prime suspect. And it would be very difficult to prove one's innocence. In the past, many innocent police officers have fallen victim of that simple trap, but the eventual result was that all property handed to the police was treated with great caution and respect. Meticulous records were kept with double-checking where necessary.

Another means of framing police officers became prevalent during the left-wing inspired riots and demonstrations of the mid-1960s; particularly at Grosvenor Square in London. This is the location of the American Embassy and in 1968 it witnessed one of the most violent anti-war riots ever experienced. Apart from the general mayhem, some demonstrators stained their faces, hands and clothes with red dye, tomato juice or some other colouring, get themselves photographed by the television cameras or press, or even by their own colleagues, and then claim they had been beaten up by police officers wielding batons. False claims of police brutality were rife and were usually believed by the public who read the press reports or watched television coverage. Another trick by the demonstrators was to throw marbles on the ground so that police horses lost their footing and their confidence.

Whilst incidents of this kind are pre-planned and undertaken with cruel and malicious intent, it is a fact that innocent people can find themselves charged with crimes through no one's fault or evil intent. One within my experience was a 22-year-old university student called Alexander Lennox.

With long hair, jeans and an apparent sloppy or very casual attitude to life, he was from a decent home and, when the incident occurred, he was on his way back to Leeds University after a weekend at home with his parents in Aidensfield. He had secured a lift to Ashfordly where he was waiting to catch a bus to York, that being his connection with the Leeds service. With his long, unruly hair, scruffy appearance and a haversack on his back, he was standing alone in the darkness at the York bus stop in Ashfordly. There were fifteen minutes or so before his bus was due and behind the bus stop was a waist-high stone wall so he decided to take the weight off his feet and sit on top of it. He hoisted himself on to the wall and sat dangling his feet, with his haversack at his side. For a while, he was completely alone. As he waited, however, a group of eight or nine noisy teenagers arrived, boys and girls.

With bottles of beer and lager, haversacks on their backs and armed with transistor radios, they halted at the stop to await the York bus. They acknowledged Alex, but he did not know who they were – listening to their chatter, they appeared to be from York and had been to an afternoon party in Ashfordly. They had been drinking and were in a very boisterous but not an angry or threatening mood; they were singing to the music from the transistor, cheering at times, telling bawdy jokes, drinking from bottles which kept appearing from their haversacks and generally being very loud and almost intimidating, shouting their jokes and singing their songs.

Then one of them decided to dispose of an empty lager bottle. He launched it as if he was throwing a hand grenade and flung it into the darkness behind the bus stop. There was a crash of glass – it had either gone through a window or into a greenhouse. Then another youth decided to do the same with his empty bottle. Another crash of glass to a round of cheers . . . a great sport had just been discovered but in fact no more bottles were thrown.

In the early stages of this development, a resident in a flat overlooking the garden that contained the greenhouse peeped out of his window and, beneath the street lamp at the bus stop, had seen the group of boisterous youngsters. He heard the crash of glass, twice. He rang the police to report at least two cases of malicious damage by a group of yobs who were, at that very moment, causing a disturbance at the York road bus stop.

By chance, a road traffic division patrol car with two officers on board was cruising around the outskirts of Ashfordly and it immediately raced to the scene. It was rapidly supported by the Ashfordly Section general purpose vehicle which was also patrolling the town with two officers on board. None of the youngsters had any idea the police had been called and it was therefore with some surprise on their part that two police vehicles with flashing lights suddenly confronted them and contained them. Four burly officers leapt out and ordered the teenagers to stand still as they were all under arrest for causing a breach of the peace. There was the added possibility that they would also be charged with committing malicious damage. In this unexpected way, Alexander Lennox suddenly found himself being marched with the rest of the mob towards Ashfordly Police Station where the youths and girls would be processed.

'Look,' he protested, 'it's nothing to do with me. I'm not with them. I'm just waiting for a bus. . . .'

'They all say that, sonny,' responded one of the officers. 'We've got a witness . . . he saw you chucking those bottles about and causing a disturbance. He had a grandstand view, and he's not senile or blind. He's a good witness. You're all typical yobbos. Come along, you're going to Ashfordly Police Station where you'll all be charged and, if you behave yourselves in the meantime, you'll be bailed out to appear at court sometime in the future.'

'Look, I'm not with these people . . . I'm not . . . ask them,' tried Alex, in desperation.

'It's up to you to prove your innocence, young man; we've all the evidence that's necessary to prove guilt by all of you. We say one guilty, all guilty, but it's up to the court to decide who's guilty and who's innocent. I would add we don't take kindly to specially fabricated false alibis that pervert the course of justice. We have a good witness who saw you all misbehaving . . . we saw you, too, all of you, congregating at the bus stop and shouting a lot. We'll have you all for aiding and abetting one another. . . .'

And so it was that Alex found himself taken into Ashfordly Police Station under arrest, stripped of his personal belongings, placed in a cell and told he would be charged with one of several public order offences whilst aiding and abetting two cases of malicious damage. Even though he continued to protest his innocence, his pleas fell on deaf ears. 'One guilty, all guilty' muttered one of the police officers.

By chance, I was undertaking a late evening patrol around my Aidensfield beat and popped into Ashfordly Police Station to drop off some reports for onward transmission to sub-divisional headquarters. I arrived just as Sergeant Bairstow, the night duty sergeant whose patch was normally Brantsford, was bailing out the troublemakers.

The arresting officers had left to resume their patrolling, and the small station was full of rather subdued teenagers, all waiting for the bailing-out procedures to be completed. I spotted Alex among them, at that time being unaware of the drama that had resulted in his arrest.

'Trouble, Alex?' I took him aside as the final ones were being bailed.

'Yes, Mr Rhea. But I've not done anything. Honest. But nobody will believe me.'

'So what's the story?'

He told me his side of the story, but he had no idea how the police had known about the incident nor did he know any of the York youngsters. I was tempted to believe him, but it seemed the police had already made their enquiries

117

and come to a conclusion that incriminated him.

I assured him I would try and find out more about it, but things didn't look very good for him. I asked one or two of the others if they knew Alex, or if he was one of their group, and they shook their heads. 'Never seen him before; he was waiting at the bus stop when we got there,' said one of them.

'He wasn't with you at all?'

'No, he wasn't with us. I told the fuzz, but they said they didn't believe me. They had a good solid witness who said we were all involved. We weren't, it was just two of us who threw the bottles – mebbe we were making a bit of a noise, but we weren't fighting, or being obnoxious or anything . . . just enjoying ourselves, singing a bit and mebbe shouting out jokes and things, like you do after a party.'

'This needs a little more investigation,' I said. 'Leave it with me.'

Due to all the turmoil, Alex missed his bus to York and so he had to telephone his parents from a kiosk and ask them to collect him. When they asked for an explanation, he said he would explain on the way home. However, there was a much more serious aspect to this event that meant Alex had another major problem. Although still attending university, he had been accepted for training as an RAF officer at Cranwell, the Royal Air Force College. His acceptance would depend upon the result of his finals, but there was another condition: no one with a criminal record would be accepted as an RAF officer. His involvement with this comparatively minor incident would therefore have serious consequences to his future career. He told me this as he waited for his parents to collect him.

'Tell them I'll help all I can,' I promised. 'Not just for you, but for some of these others. Although I'm in the job, I think those officers have over-reacted, or their witness has over-stated the case. Ask your mother to get in touch with me.'

'Thanks, Mr Rhea.'

Mrs Lennox was a top criminal lawyer whose work took her to the assizes and quarter sessions throughout the north of England, including the Crown Courts of Manchester and Liverpool which had been established only some ten years earlier. A feisty blonde lady in her early fifties with a love for loud classical music and Labrador dogs, she had a reputation for securing acquittals in some very difficult cases. And now, I felt, she would have to exercise her skills for the sake of her son.

Before I left Ashfordly Police Station, I jotted down the names, ages and addresses of the York group – perhaps I shouldn't have done that because it might have infringed some internal rule of confidentiality, but I felt Alex needed all the help he could get. I would ring Eltering Police Station from home to get the name and address of the witness who had sent the police to this incident – at night, all calls were automatically routed to Eltering if Ashfordly is not staffed. Ashfordly had not been staffed when the witness had called and so it had gone through to Eltering. As a result, Sergeant Bairstow had been brought in from Brantsford to deal with the arrested youngsters.

First thing the following morning, I obtained details of that witness – a Mr Alfred George Chivers of Flat 2, York

House, 19, York Road, Ashfordly, a retired accountant aged seventy-two. No one queried my reason for wanting his name – after all, I had been on duty in Aidensfield during that minor disturbance in Ashfordly even if I had not been directly involved, so it was logical I might have to interview Mr Chivers. That was the impression I managed to achieve without telling any untruths.

As expected, I received a phone call early next morning from Mrs Lennox who had been led by Alex to understand I might be able to help in his predicament. I confirmed that and said I would come and talk to her. She suggested 10.30 at her house. Alex would also be present. I agreed. When I arrived, I was shown into her smart, airy lounge where a coffee table was already laid with cups. She showed me to a chair and poured coffee whilst Alex handed me a plate of chocolate biscuits.

'Alex has told me what happened,' she said. 'For the record, Mr Rhea, I believe him. I know he is my son and I understand how protective parents can become in these circumstances, but with my training and experience, I can sense the truth when I hear it.'

'That's what I felt last night, Mrs Lennox, when I chanced to arrive at Ashfordly Police Station. I must admit I thought those officers – some of whom were not local by the way – were rather heavy-handed.'

'It could be argued they were merely responding to the evidence of the witness who called the police. Some witnesses can be a serious problem, Mr Rhea, especially if they are biased and especially if they always believe their own eyes. I need this person to appear in the witness box where I can cross-examine him with all the strength I can muster.'

'I have his name and address,' I said, handing her a piece of paper. 'And it contains details of all those York youngsters. I thought you might need it.'

'I won't ask whether you are allowed to give me this, but in any case I could make my own enquiries to find the witness – not many people live in flats behind that bus stop. But thanks, this will make my task much easier – we might even get this matter sorted out without a court appearance.'

And so it transpired. Mrs Lennox interviewed Mr Chivers, the witness, but he could only say he had heard noises at the bus stop and two instances of smashed glass. Quite understandably, he thought vandals were responsible – and they were right opposite his flat. But he could not identify precisely who had thrown the bottles. Not satisfied with this modest result, Mrs Lennox went to York where she traced and interviewed all the youngsters.

Every one of them confirmed that Alex was not involved in either their rowdy behaviour or the bottle throwing. She obtained the names of the bottle throwers and said she would now present her findings to the superintendent at Malton, under whose command Ashfordly lay.

Not surprisingly, all charges against Alex and most of the others were dropped, although two York youngsters were officially cautioned for causing malicious damage. No one was either prosecuted or cautioned for any public order offences – the two 'malicious damage' cautions arose because both lads admitted their guilt.

My part in all this was never publicized or made known

to the authorities, but Mrs Lennox sent me a nice letter of thanks, saying that Alex was now going ahead with his ambition to become an RAF officer.

Chapter 8

Duty Bound to Find the Truth

Debbie Brookes was thirteen years old and the eldest of a family of four – two more girls and a boy who was the youngest. She lived with her parents and siblings in a council house in Aidensfield. Her father worked for the Highways Department of the County Council. Her mother was a part-time barmaid and waitress in the local pub. All the children were well mannered, well turned out and well behaved.

Debbie was a tall and very elegant girl with long, reddish hair often tied back in a pony-tail with a brightly coloured ribbon.

She had freckles too and a ready smile which often gave her the appearance of being cheeky and confident. She was certainly confident but no one could call her cheeky because she was a polite youngster who could mingle easily with adults and children of all ages. In all sorts of ways, she was an ideal daughter and a friend of many in the village.

One of her activities in Aidensfield was running errands for the elderly and infirm. In some cases, her 'customers' insisted on paying Debbie a few shillings for her trouble, but she did not canvas money from anyone; she was quite happy to run errands for no reward because she liked helping other people. She had a list of regulars for whom she would do shopping, collect newspapers, clean windows, tidy up indoors, shake rugs, sweep paths, collect fallen leaves, or even clean cars.

Because some of these people paid her a few shillings she always had pocket money, most of which she saved in a small money box on her bedroom mantelpiece.

Then an elderly couple, Fred and Grace Gilpin, moved into one of the bungalows opposite the church. Both were retired, the husband having worked for Leeds City Council while his wife had worked in a city centre ladies' clothing store. They were a decent couple who wished to retire to a village lifestyle in Aidensfield and they seemed to settle in very quickly. Both were keen Anglicans who patronized the village church and very soon after their arrival they began to play an active part in other village affairs. They helped by being on the committee of the village hall, running an afternoon tea-and-talk session for the over-sixties, doing charity work and helping with things like the annual garden fête and flower show. Unlike some incomers to other villages, they did not try to change things in Aidensfield, being content to serve the existing community in all sorts of simple and rather gentle ways. Frederick was a tall, smart, grey-haired gentleman with a splendid moustache who often wore a dark suit – a reminder of his days working for Leeds Council. Grace was equally smart in her tweed skirts, blouses and cardigans – never did anyone catch sight of her in slacks or jeans.

Then Grace fell off a step-ladder in the garden whilst trying to reach a climbing rose which needed pruning and she broke an ankle. She was seen by Dr McGee of Elsinby and treated in Elsinby Cottage Hospital where her ankle was put in plaster and she was issued with a pair of crutches. This seriously curtailed her activities in and around the village and Frederick also found his outings became very much restricted because he had to stay at home and care for his wife. It was at this point that a friend suggested that if they needed any help with the shopping and other minor jobs, then Debbie Brookes was just the girl. The Gilpins thought it was a good idea. The same friend therefore approached Debbie to ask if she could accommodate the Gilpins' modest requirements during her busy after-school or weekends and the obliging teenager said she was happy to be of assistance; she would call on the Gilpins. During my frequent patrols of Aidensfield both on duty and off, I would often see the cheerful young redhead going about the village on her various errands. Here was one teenager who had no trouble occupying herself when not at school.

Then one blustery April Saturday, Debbie's parents received a phone call from Frederick Gilpin to say he had to travel into York on business so could Debbie please call on Mrs Gilpin later this morning as she had a list of things she needed from the Aidensfield Stores? Mr Gilpin added that if his wife did not respond to the doorbell, she would probably be in the garden, sitting and reading in the wooden cabin he had bought for her. Debbie should go into the house which would not be locked and continue through to the garden where Mrs Gilpin would be sitting. She would then explain her requirements. Debbie did as she had been requested, visiting Aidensfield Stores with Mrs Gilpin's shopping list. As the Gilpins had an account with the shop, Debbie did not take any money; the Gilpins would settle up at the month end, as they always did. Debbie returned to the house with a full basket, went back into the house and let Mrs Gilpin know she had fulfilled her task. Mrs Gilpin said her husband would empty the basket and put the groceries on the shelves of the kitchen and into the various cupboards, and she then gave Debbie a half-crown. Debbie left the house shortly after twelve noon and went home.

I became aware of those movements by Debbie because at six o'clock that evening I received a phone call from Frederick Gilpin. I had just finished my cooked tea and was preparing to continue the second half of that day's patrolling duty. I was due to finish at 10 p.m.

'Can you call in, Mr Rhea? It's a very delicate matter.'

'Yes, of course. What time would be suitable?'

'Now?'

'Fine,' I agreed. 'I'll be there in ten minutes.'

When I arrived, the brisk wind almost whipped the van door from my hand. The forecourt of their house seemed to be quite exposed and I almost lost my grip on the door handle; then, when Mr Gilpin responded to the doorbell, he had a struggle to hold the door open. The wind was clearly something of a nuisance and I noticed it was bringing down new blossom from the early flowering trees in their garden.

I was admitted and the door almost slammed behind me. I was shown into the Gilpins' sitting room where a coal fire was roaring due to the wind outside. The couple were having a sherry each before settling down to their evening meal. I declined because I was driving my police Mini-van but did accept a still orange drink.

'So how can I help you?' I asked.

'As I said on the phone, Mr Rhea, it is a very delicate matter and the last thing we want to do is to get anyone into trouble without due cause. But I believe in nipping trouble in the bud before it gets out of hand.'

'I understand,' I nodded in agreement as he prepared himself to break some bad news to me.

'We have had a thief in the house, Mr Rhea. Today.'

'Oh dear, that's nasty. So what's been stolen?'

'Money, Mr Rhea. A pound note.'

'From where?' was my next question.

'The small table in our front lobby. It was for the insurance man, he always collects it from there – it's for an endowment policy. He calls once a month.'

'So when did it disappear, I need the precise times?' Now I had opened my notebook and was recording the salient facts of the crime.

'I placed it there about ten o'clock this morning, before I went to York, and he came at about half-past three this afternoon. It had gone when he arrived.'

'You said it was in the front lobby. I didn't notice any sign of a break-in when I arrived just now.'

'No, Mr Rhea, we left the door unlocked. Grace prefers the front door to be left unlocked when she's alone, in case she has to call in anyone to help her. And with her broken ankle, she's not very mobile just now.'

'So where were you, Mrs Gilpin? While your husband was in York?'

'Outside in the garden, Mr Rhea. It was a lovely sunny day, if a little breezy, but I was in my cabin where it was sheltered and warm. Frederick had prepared a tray with my lunch – a salad and some fruit, and a flask of coffee – so I was quite content with my book. I could sit and be comfortable without struggling around the house on crutches.'

'So you would not be able to see that table in the front lobby.'

'Oh no, but there has never been a need to worry about thieves sneaking in. Not in Aidensfield. We've always left our money there for Norman, that's Norman Taylor from Milthorpe, our insurance man. We've never lost any before.'

'So the money was there when you left for York, Mr Gilpin – how did you notice its absence?'

Mrs Gilpin spoke. 'Norman came about half-past three, Mr Rhea, which is his usual time. I heard him open the front door, but then he came through the kitchen to find me in the cabin – he knew I'd be there. He apologized for interrupting me, but said he would collect the money next time on his rounds.'

'He knew the amount to collect?'

'Yes, I told him it was a pound note and that it was ready for him in the lobby, but he said it wasn't there.'

'He was sure about that?'

'Yes, Mr Rhea. Quite sure. I went to have a look, not easy with my crutches, but I made it. And it was not there. I wondered if Frederick had forgotten to put it out, with him having to go to York, but Norman said it didn't matter, he'd collect it next time. I didn't have enough money on me, you see, Frederick had taken most of our housekeeping to York in case he needed any cash for car-parking, lunch and so on.'

'So did you hear anyone come into the house?' was my next question.

'Only that girl,' said Mrs Gilpin, and now I detected a new sharpness in her voice. Her severe tone told me she was accusing someone.

'Which girl?'

'That red-haired girl of the Brookes, Debbie.'

'Ah. So why did she come in?'

'Frederick asked her to. I wanted some groceries from Aidensfield Stores and so he rang Debbie this morning and asked if she would collect them for me. We have an account there, Mr Rhea, and so no money was involved. She came about twelve noon as near as I can tell.'

'Through the front door?'

'Yes, Frederick told her to walk straight in and through to the kitchen and then into the garden where I would provide her with a shopping list. She went off with the list and came back with a basketful of things. I gave her a half-crown for her trouble.'

'And did anyone else enter the house?'

'No, Mr Rhea. I would have known. Even when I'm in the garden, I can hear the front door opening and closing, and especially so today with all these gusts of wind, banging doors. She was the only caller, Mr Rhea.'

'She's been doing errands around the village for a long time,' I said in Debbie's defence. 'I've never had any reports of any kind of irregularity.'

'That is why we used her, Mr Rhea. She was recommended by friends.'

'Hmm. This is not easy.' I did not want to interview Debbie as an accused person when she might not be responsible, but from what the Gilpins told me, she seemed to be the prime suspect – the only suspect, in fact. I would have to speak to the insurance man, too, to obtain his version of events and would also have to ask questions around Aidensfield to ascertain whether anyone had noticed people calling at the Gilpins' house during those critical hours.

Things did look rather black for Debbie and if she had taken the money, she must be identified as the thief and prosecuted. If she was innocent of any wrongdoing, however, an interview by the police could destroy her self-confidence.

I was very aware of the old saying that thrown mud always sticks. I knew I must tread carefully with this one. I did not want anyone outside this house to suspect the girl was a thief if she was innocent – vicious rumours could spread like wildfire around a small community like Aidensfield.

'I need to have a close look at the place from where it vanished,' I said, wondering what I should really do about this accusation. Like many police officers, I had a sixth sense about reported crime and in my experience, this allegation did not ring true. Only two people had called at the house during the material times – I did not doubt Mrs Gilpin's testimony on that point. One had been invited into the house to conduct a small errand on behalf of the Gilpins, and the other was the insurance man, a regular caller for whom the premiums were left in a very accessible place. I knew both and considered neither to be a thief. If a sneak thief had opened the door and noticed the money, then Mrs Gilpin would have known – her inner doors would have slammed in the gusts and that had not happened, except when Debbie had called. Debbie had closed the front door and then opened the others *en route* to the garden. And they'd slammed again when the insurance man had called – and he had opened them for Mrs Gilpin. She wanted them open so she could hear if anyone came in, but had nothing with which to prop them open. She was therefore convinced no one else had entered by the front door. I found myself coming to the conclusion that I must stage a modest re-enactment of the crime.

'Mr Gilpin,' I said, 'can you help me? I believe you placed the pound note on the table in the lobby?'

'Yes, before I went to York.'

'Can you do it again please? To show me precisely where it was. And Mrs Gilpin, can you go and sit in your cabin, and leave the kitchen door and any others exactly as they were whilst Mr Gilpin was in York?'

It took a few minutes for Mrs Gilpin to hobble out to the garden, but once she was settled, I stood in the kitchen for a moment or two to absorb the entire scenario. The door into the garden was standing open and so was the internal kitchen door which led into the entrance hall; I could see into the hall and the lobby beyond – all the doors (including the one leading into the garden) were open except the front door.

I walked into the entrance hall. It was spacious with a red and green tiled floor and couple of rugs, while the door between it and the lobby had a coloured glass window to permit the light to enter. Now that door was standing open. Inside the hall was a round mahogany table bearing a large pot plant thick with variegated pale green leaves and reddish flowers; I had no idea what it was but it looked splendid. The walls bore several prints of local beauty spots, and there was a mirror over an umbrella stand that stood before the disused fireplace. The fire was laid as if awaiting someone to ignite it – but it was probably never lit. A typical entrance hall, I felt. The lobby or porch was very small, however, again with a red and green tiled floor; the front door was solid with a letter box and there were two side windows each with clear glass. On one side there stood a narrow oak table beneath the window on the left as one entered through the front door. It bore a large vase of tulips and nothing else.

'Now,' I said to Mr Gilpin, 'show me where you placed the money. Can we use a real note, just as you did earlier?'

'Of course,' he said, taking out his wallet. He extracted a crisp £1 note.

'Was it folded on the table? Or lying flat? Or weighted down?'

'No, I just placed it on the table, near that vase. It was flat, like this,' and he placed the note on the table. 'We always leave it like that for the insurance man. We've never had trouble before.'

'Thanks,' I said. 'Now, open the front door as if you were that girl coming in . . . perhaps if you went out through the back, round the house and came in through the front door, to replicate her arrival?'

'Yes, right.'

And off he went. It took a minute or two from him to walk around the house from back to front then I heard him tap on the front door and shout, 'Is it all right now, Mr Rhea?'

'Yes,' I said. 'Come in.'

And as he opened the door, a gust of wind slammed all the doors in the house – and blew the £1 note from the table. As he closed the front door and joined me, he saw the money was missing.

'Right,' I said. 'The money has gone, but where? Now, let's follow Debbie's steps.' We moved into the house, opening the doors that now stood open and eventually reached Mrs Gilpin in her cabin.

'The money wasn't stolen,' Frederick said to his wife before I could tell her. 'It blew off the table when she entered – it's still gusty outside, but I've no idea where the money went.'

'There are now two pound notes hiding somewhere in the house,' I said. 'We'd better find them, if only to be absolutely sure that's what happened.'

Frederick Gilpin and I searched the rooms between the lobby and the kitchen exit to the garden, and we found both notes. One was in the fireplace, lodged between two of the decorative logs, and the other was in the large potted flower in the entrance hall. At first glance, it looked just like one of its leaves.

'I don't know how to thank you, Mr Rhea,' said Mr Gilpin. 'I could have so easily accused that young girl of stealing. . . .'

'But you didn't — no one else knows of her near miss! I'm pleased you didn't approach her directly and accuse her to her face as some people would have done. But, as they say, all's well that ends well.'

As a gesture of his relief at the outcome of this minor investigation, Mr Gilpin donated both £1 notes to a police charity. I said I would pay them into the Widows and Orphans Fund — and gave him a receipt, just to be sure I didn't get accused to stealing them!

Chapter 9

Outward Bound

With thoughts of boundaries in mind, it is correct to say that a large percentage of a rural police officer's duty did not involve either crime or police work. Quite frequently, we would find ourselves dealing with matters more of a social nature than anything that was officially part of our work. Once a woman hailed me with a cheery wave as I patrolled along Briggsby main street. I did not recognize her and, to my knowledge, I had never met her previously. As I responded by waving back, I noticed her fine detached house had a 'For Sale' sign in its front garden. Then she called to me.

'Excuse me, Constable, but could you spare me a minute of your time?'

'Yes of course.'

'How fortunate that you should be walking past at this very moment,' she oozed. 'I need someone to help me.'

'Well, if I can help, I will.'

'Thank you, but do come in, the kettle is already boiling and I can chat to you over a cup of tea or coffee – that's if you've got the time.'

'I've always time for a cup of coffee!' I smiled.

'Good, I need a break. Please excuse my dress – I'm packing in readiness for moving, I've sold the house you see. I'm Dorothy Frankland, by the way. Mrs.'

She led me through the large, airy house via a central corridor and, as I glanced into the adjoining rooms, I noticed everything seemed to be packed in crates, boxes and tea-chests. They occupied almost every empty space on the floors of all the rooms and passageways. The walls were bare too and all but two of the rooms – the lounge she used at night and her bedroom I guessed – had no curtains. Evidently, she was soon to quit this house.

'When are you moving?' I asked, as she led me to the kitchen.

'The day after tomorrow,' she said. 'I'm selling up and going to live in Spain where it's warmer. They're coming for my furniture tomorrow so there's still a lot to do. I shall stay with friends before catching my ship. Besides, I have family out there. Since my husband died, I've felt the need for lots of sunshine and a more relaxed way of life. The new owners move in next week. I have to ensure the house is empty by Monday at the latest.'

She made the coffee whilst chatting to me and then we sat down on a couple of stools with a tin of chocolate biscuits placed between us. I was still not sure why she had invited me in.

'Eat as many biscuits as you can, I have to clear everything as soon as possible. I don't want any food left over. Now, you'll be wondering why I called you.'

'Well, yes,' I admitted. 'Perhaps you need a hand lifting something? I don't mind doing that sort of thing if it will help. . . .'

'It's kind of you, but I've had expert packers in and help from lots of volunteers in the village. And besides, the exercise keeps me warm, I've no heating in the house just now and it's rather chilly outside and inside. Now, it's Queenie. She's the problem. She has disappeared, vanished from the face of the earth. Or vanished from this house to be more precise. She never leaves the area around the house or the house itself, never.'

'Queenie?'

'My cat, Mr Rhea. I've had her for years – ten years or so – and I cannot leave her behind. I must not abandon her, she is far too precious. I have to find her . . . poor Queenie. She doesn't enjoy all the upheaval. I think she knows something awful is going to happen to her. Cats are like that, Mr Rhea, very sensitive to change and receptive to the moods of their owners. Then they sulk as they go away and hide.'

I added my story. 'Our cat seems to know when we're getting ready for a holiday. She hides in the hope we won't put her into a cattery or leave her with friends. We usually find her before we go, but obviously she's never happy about us leaving – and she does seem to know what's happening.'

'Exactly the same with Queenie, Mr Rhea. She doesn't

like change and I am sure she can read my thoughts. Even so, I doubt if she knows we're heading for Spain, or how important it is for me to be completely ready at the appointed time.'

'So how can I help?'

'Well, I wondered if the police might have a system for looking for lost cats. . . .'

'It's not within our range of duties, Mrs Frankland; lost people, yes, but cats, well, no. We might look for straying cattle because they're a danger to road users and we might even publicize a missing dog. Cats are rather different – they're prone to wandering anyway, especially the toms. Certainly we can't carry out a physical search for a lost cat – we don't have the manpower – but we will enter a description of her in our records in case someone reports seeing her somewhere. I know you're short of time but local newspapers often carry adverts for missing cats.'

'I can't wait that long, Constable. I must do something immediately.'

'Could she be trapped somewhere in the house?'

'To be honest, I have no idea. I think if she was, I would have heard her calling.'

'Well, if you do think she's trapped somewhere in the house – under the floorboards or wherever – then the RSPCA might be the best people to help.'

'But that would all take time . . . ripping up floorboards and so on. I can't think of any way she would do that, Constable. There are no holes she could use to hide like that.'

'It's amazing where cats can get to. But if you were

absolutely sure she was trapped somewhere in the building, the Fire Brigade might help – or perhaps a local carpenter? They'd respond quickly, but they could cause some damage to your house just before you are due to leave, especially if it's a case of taking up floorboards or knocking down walls.'

'Oh dear, I don't know what to suggest, this could be a major problem, couldn't it? I do hope I don't have to leave Queenie behind . . . it would break my heart.'

'Have you asked around the village? Put a notice in the shop and post office?'

'Not yet, I've only just discovered her absence. She was here for breakfast this morning and I've just noticed she's missing. She's not in her usual haunts. I had to drive into Ashfordly to get something for lunch and when I got back, I noticed she'd gone. She's always around the house, Mr Rhea, she's not one for roaming across the fields, or going into the woods, or even visiting other houses or farms. She's a female and therefore very much a home cat.'

'Perhaps if she's hiding she could have got into a packing case, or gone into the loft.'

'I think she must be in the house, Mr Rhea. But with so much packing to do, I don't have the time to go searching every nook and cranny and besides, if I get near her, she might go deeper into hiding.'

'Would food tempt her out?'

'I'm sure it would, but if I was in bed or elsewhere when she emerged, she would eat it and go straight back into her new hiding place. . . .'

'I think you need to circulate her description around the village and nearby farms, just to be sure she isn't at someone else's house . . . is she distinctive?'

'Very, Mr Rhea. She's a Manx cat, a tabby with white underparts, and as I am sure you know, Manx cats have no tail. They have longer than normal rear legs which makes them look rather like a rabbit . . . you can't miss her, Mr Rhea. She's wearing a red leather collar with my name on it.'

'My grandfather had Manx cats on his farm, they were very gentle and faithful cats, Mrs Frankland, even if they did look a bit odd.'

'One gets accustomed to their appearance, Mr Rhea. Well, I mustn't stand here talking all afternoon when there is packing to be done.'

'Will it help if I have a wander around the house? To try and find her hiding place? I'm happy to do that for you. After all, policemen are used to searching for stolen goods, drugs and even children who are hiding. Those techniques might find your cat and I have no pressing engagements right now.'

'Well, yes, provided you don't think the entire house is a tip! Most of the rooms are packed with boxes and crates. The curtains are down, the wardrobes and furniture have been dismantled where possible . . . it's dreadful, Mr Rhea. I'm beginning to wish I'd never come up with this idea.'

'Are they sealed? Those crates and boxes which are complete?'

'Yes, she couldn't sneak into one of those.'

'I think any unsealed packing cases and other boxes are the ideal place to start. Show me to the first bedroom and I'll wander around looking for hiding places while you continue packing. And I'll alert people in the village during my rounds. If I don't find her, then it will be time to call in the experts — the RSPCA or Fire Brigade. Now, does she respond to any noises? Like you tapping her plate when it's supper time or scraping a plate — food noises.'

'She always comes running when she hears me opening a tin of cat food — the noise of the tin being opened makes her run towards me.'

'Then I shall go armed with a tin opener and a few cans of cat food . . . but don't tell the sergeant!'

And so began my great cat hunt.

I knew that a cat seeking a hiding place would make good use of any convenient hole, even the chimney or loft-door if it was open. Open drawers, cupboards, wardrobes, suitcases, spaces in bedding or other soft furnishings, gaps behind large items of furniture or even behind those packed cases and boxes . . . all were fair game to a determined cat.

Having had to search houses for drugs, stolen property and even the carcase of a long-dead baby, I thought I knew how to operate. I had to be thorough but systematic, and I hadn't to neglect even the smallest and most unlikely hiding place. After all, I was dealing with a cat, not a human!

I knew of a cat that had somehow squeezed into its owner's suitcase just before he had closed it — and he had found it on board ship when he started to unpack his clothes. That caused immense problems so far as the official period of quarantine was concerned — man and cat had somehow bypassed all the necessary embarkation and Customs controls. And it wasn't his fault — but you can't blame a cat!

To complete my search, I told Mrs Frankland I would start with the loft and work my way through all the bedrooms, closing the doors when my search was complete to ensure that Queenie didn't bypass me and bolt into one of the areas already searched. Then I would continue downstairs.

I kept popping out to my van to see if my radio was calling me for any emergency, and then moved it on to the drive where I reckoned that if I increased the volume to maximum, I would hear my call-sign if control wanted to contact me.

It took over an hour to complete my search of the loft and bedrooms, but I was satisfied the cat was not there in spite of my making food noises with cans and opener. Mrs Frankland was working in the dining room, finishing her packing of some crockery and so I adopted the same technique as I had upstairs.

I searched inch by inch, room by room, checking every gap in which a determined cat might have hidden – all with no result. I had not found any loose floorboards or holes in the wall, and the chimney showed no sign of a cat having scrambled up – there was no deposit of soot in any of the hearths.

I was baffled. Then Mrs Frankland said I looked roasted in spite of the chilly weather outdoors and she said she had put the kettle on yet again for another brew, and more chocolate biscuits. It was hot and tiring work, we realized. As we sat in her kitchen with me enjoying the biscuits and doing my best not to let any of them go to waste, I asked,

'Have you any outbuildings?'

'Not any more,' she told me. 'I had a nice garden shed with a small veranda at one end, but I couldn't take it with me. I gave it to one of my helpers – I said he could have it for nothing if he dismantled it and took it away. So he did.'

'And there's nowhere outside where Queenie might hide?'

'Just the garage, but I've already looked in there. She's not in the car, Mr Rhea, or asleep among any of the other things I've got in there.'

'Do you mind if I have a look? She might have crept in while we've been searching the house.'

I wasn't telling the whole truth, of course, because I didn't want to suggest Mrs Frankland had not done a proper job, but if there's one thing a cat likes on a cold day it is a warm place to sleep. The heating was off in the house, there were no fires and Mrs Frankland was not using her oven and I'd even checked the airing cupboard and hot water cylinder. We were warm through our physical efforts.

I asked, 'You said you drove into Ashfordly this morning, Mrs Frankland? Was it in your own car?'

'Yes, of course. Why?'

'Come with me,' I smiled. 'I think I might know where Queenie has got to! And bring your car keys.'

We walked around to the garage and when we got inside, I suggested we closed the doors just in case Queenie tried to bolt away if she was rudely awakened. Then I unlocked the car, pulled the release catch for the bonnet and went to the front of the car to fully raise it. And there, sleeping on the warm block of the engine, somehow finding room among the wires, plugs and cables, was a tabby cat without a tail.

'She hasn't a tail to keep her warm,' I smiled.

'Oh, Mr Rhea, I am so relieved, so, so relieved ... Queenie, come along and don't go doing that sort of trick again!'

And so Queenie was lifted out of the engine compartment and carried into the house, hopefully to be contained until Mrs Frankland's departure. She wanted to give me something for my efforts but I refused – after all, I had done a useful job and eaten lots of her chocolate biscuits. I left Mrs Frankland overjoyed at finding her cat and said that if she wanted to show her appreciation she could donate something either to a police charity or an animal welfare fund.

'I'll do that,' she promised.

I went to my van, settled in the seat and then the radio burbled to life with my call sign. 'Delta Alpha Two Four, go ahead,' I responded.

'Where are you, Nick?' It was Alf Ventress from Ashfordly.

'Briggsby, Alf, just completed a foot patrol of the village.'

'Well, we've been trying to contact you for ages – get yourself down to the road between Brantsford and Crampton. Fast as you can. Location near Holly Bush Farm. Sarge is down there along with PC Foxton and PC Warner – he's not best pleased you weren't answering your calls.'

'I've been helping a distraught lady locate a missing cat,' I said. 'It took longer than I thought.'

'Well, your experience with animals should be useful, Nick. There's a bull running loose on the road near Holly Bush and they're trying to round it up. The owner and his farmhands are already there, but it's causing traffic mayhem and has already head-butted a car and caused a bus to swerve into a field. On your way, mate.'

'On my way it is, Alf. Delta Alpha Two Four out. Do I need my bullfighting outfit?'

He didn't reply.

By the time I arrived at that incident, all traffic had been halted whilst the frightened bull had taken refuge in a small copse of mature trees at the edge of a small lay-by at the side of the road. It stood there staring at the men who were trying to coax it into a field the gate of which had been opened especially for its use. Normally, it is not wise to drive straying animals into the nearest field because they might spread disease among those that normally occupy it, but in this case, the field belonged to the owner of the bull, Ted Kitchener.

As we all stood around with traffic halted at each side of the incident, there was a welcome respite from its motor vehicle charging technique but the question of how to persuade it to leave its barricade of stout trees was not easy. Somehow, the frightened bull had to be persuaded to leave its haven and head for the open gate. Any sudden move on our part would send it charging out of the trees and probably back among the stationary motor traffic where mayhem could result. Another option was to shoot the bull, but I knew Ted would resist that course – bulls are valuable animals but they cannot be driven as one might drive a sheep. A few waving arms will persuade a sheep to take a different course but to wave one's arms at a bull, in an attempt to divert it from a chosen path was asking for severe trouble. Persuasion seemed the answer. But how?

Then something strange happened. Somewhere in the line of stationary lorries and cars parked beyond the open farm gate, a hooter sounded.

It was what the police would call a multi-tone horn, very popular in the 1960s. Some enthusiasts fitted two-tone horns to their vehicles but these were illegal because they sounded too much like the horns used on emergency vehicles. Only certain specified vehicles could be fitted with bells, gongs, sirens and two-tone horns, but the legislation did not outlaw multi-tone horns. And so yet more enthusiasts fitted horns that played tunes or created jingles.

However, one of the parked motorists was clearly fed up with waiting for the problem to be cleared and probably had no idea what was causing the traffic hold-up. As he pipped his peculiar multi-tone horn, it caused the bull to lift its head as it listened, and then it began to trot towards the sound. And, as the driver continued to hoot, clearly without being able to see, the bull left its cover among the trees and was now trotting rapidly towards him. It was not charging angrily; rather it was trotting out of curiosity. Ted Kitchener responded rapidly because he could see the bull was going to trot past the open gate – and he wanted it to go through and into the field behind. Meanwhile the police just waited, trying to appease the gathering queue of motorists and all the time wondering when it was time to call in the police marksman.

From my position, I could not see which vehicle was producing the curious hooting sounds, but, as the driver persisted, so the bull trotted closer and closer, sniffing at other cars along the way. And Ted followed. And so did I because I did not have a specific task. Eventually the bull halted near the offending car, sniffed it and then stood at its side on the wide grass verge. By now, of course, a very frightened young man was sitting in the car and he had ceased hooting his special noise-maker. But now there was another stand-off with the bull standing on the verge quite calmly. However, Ted arrived at the car from the opposite side, the bull not paying him any attention because it was accustomed to having Ted around.

Ted tapped on the car window and the driver lowered it, but only a fraction.

'Can you do me a favour?' asked Ted.

'Don't you worry, mate, I'll not sound my horn again, not with that animal standing there.'

'No, I want you to pull out of the traffic and drive slowly along, tooting that horn. The bull will follow. Just down the road there's an open field – you can drive in and the bull will come after you.'

'You're joking, mate!'

'If you don't, we're all going to be here all day, waiting for the bull to do something.'

'What if it catches me?'

'Blow your horn, it must think it's a cow or something. It likes you.'

The young man took a lot of persuading, but as the bull simply stood at his side, he nodded.

'Well, if it does charge, I reckon my car will outpace it. So where's this field?'

Ted explained, suggesting the driver coaxed the bull into the field and then accelerated to leave the bull behind as he raced back to the exit. Ted would be standing by the gate to close it the moment the car had left.

And so this unlikely scenario was acted out, with me guiding the youth and his car out of the line of parked vehicles, tooting his horn as the bull wound its way through the cars and lorries to follow like a meek little lamb. He led the bull down the offside of the road, with traffic halted at the far side of the gate that lane was empty. When he spotted the open gate, he began to toot his horn as he led the bull into the empty field. Ted was already there and, as the driver entered, he pressed the accelerator and the curious horn, leaving the puzzled bull now breaking into a gallop to try and keep pace with its new found friend.

But the driver was good and the field was solid beneath the grass. As the driver led the bull away he turned sharply to leave the bull behind as he now raced for the gate. The bull was galloping after him, but the lad won. As he passed through the gateway, Ted slammed the gate shut. I must admit I thought the massive animal was going to crash through it. But it didn't. And now, of course, the soothing sound of the horn had ceased.

But the bull was contained and safe.

I halted the young driver and asked, 'Can you leave your name and address? Ted will want it, I know he'll want to thank you for what you've done, it means he did not have to have his bull shot.'

'No thanks, Officer, I'm not hanging round here a minute longer than necessary.'

And he roared away as I directed him into the road, to be followed by the other vehicles, some of whom would have no idea what had caused the hold-up.

Afterwards, I asked Ted, 'Why did your bull respond to that car horn?'

'Search me, Nick. Mebbe it sounded like one of my cows.'

Chapter 10

A Boundary Stroke

One very minor incident that was certainly within the scope of my duty resulted from a phone call from Alan Fenwick, secretary of Thackerston Cricket Club.

'Glad I caught you, Nick.' It was approaching ten o'clock one Saturday morning and I was about to embark on the day's patrolling of my beat. It was pleasant, working a day shift on a Saturday and I hoped nothing would turn up to spoil my Saturday evening off – evening and night coverage was being provided by Ashfordly Police.

Alan was manager of a large department store in Ashfordly and a thoroughly decent person; in his spare time he worked hard for the benefit of Thackerston and its small community.

'So how can I help you, Alan?'

'Somebody's broken into the cricket pavilion,' he said. 'I'm not sure what's been taken yet but I thought I'd better

call you before you disappeared into the countryside.'
Clearly, he was fairly familiar with my daily routine.

'I'll be with you in ten minutes,' I promised.

I rang Alf Ventress at Ashfordly and told him I was
heading for Thackerston to investigate a reported break-in
at the cricket pavilion.

'Remember the changes to the Theft Act, Nick,' said Alf.
'A cricket pavilion is considered a building for burglary
purposes, which means if someone has broken in, then the
crime is burglary. Not merely pavilion breaking or
attempted theft or malicious damage. That's a good one for
our crime statistics ... a burglary! We don't get many
burglaries in these parts.'

'Let's hope I can solve it,' I replied. 'I don't want an
unsolved burglary on my patch!'

'Understood; best of luck, Nick.'

Thackerston cricket field was behind the village hall,
with access along a narrow unmade lane that ran beside the
western wall of the hall. The field had been donated to the
village by a wealthy landowner for what was loosely
described as recreational purposes but it was chiefly used
for cricket matches and the annual agricultural and
horticultural show – which was held in the autumn when
the cricket season had finished. That allowed the churned-
up pitch to be restored before the next season.

For reasons I never understood, Thackerston did not
boast a football team – which was probably a good thing
because the lack of football matches helped to keep the
peace in the village so far as use of the cricket field was
concerned. Maybe the lads who would be playing football

were the same as those who played cricket – and they respected and protected their pitch.

When I arrived, Alan was waiting at the pavilion, but he had not opened the door or gone inside. I could see the smashed pane of glass in the door's window. He said he wanted to wait until I had assessed the situation. He was a jovial, well-built man in his late fifties, a calm individual who would help anyone in distress.

'So what's the story, Alan?'

'Not a lot to say really, Nick. I came down here to check things as I always do before a match. We're playing Ploatby this afternoon, and then I saw the smashed glass in that window. I thought I'd leave it until you'd inspected it – I didn't want to contaminate the crime scene! Isn't that the current jargon?'

'You did right,' I said. 'We lose a lot of evidence from scenes like this, through well-meaning helpers fiddling with things and touching places that might contain fingerprints. So let's have a closer look.'

The pavilion was built of wood with changing rooms for both teams and there was a small balcony-type area at one end where the players could have refreshments in the open air.

The pavilion was large enough to seat them under cover if they wished, or if the weather was inclement. Cricketers' wives were famous for making good, wholesome teas, and a small kitchen with storage space adjoined the balcony, albeit indoors. At the back, outside the building, were flush toilets for men and women. The whole complex was painted white and there was space for a scoreboard to be hung on the wall that faced the pitch.

I took a close look at the smashed window. It was a small pane of glass about six inches by eight and it was close to the Yale lock which secured the door. There was a neat hole through it, the glass having fallen inside the pavilion, as if someone had punched it with a fist or elbow. What had evidently happened was that someone had then reached inside and released the catch of the Yale lock. The door would have swung open to admit the perpetrator.

'You've not checked inside, Alan?'

'Not yet, no. I didn't think we kept any valuables in there – none of the team keeps his kit in here, the club's bats, balls and pads are at my house, so why bother to break in to a place like this? There's nothing worth pinching.'

'Maybe chummy broke in to have a sleep!' I smiled. 'I've known travelling tramps break into sheds and pavilions to find a bed for the night, somewhere dry and cosy. I think we'd better take a look.'

'Won't you destroy fingerprints on that lock?'

'I doubt it, Alan. The knob is very small and any prints on it will be too small for evidential purposes. Besides, if it was a break-in, the thieves will surely have left more useful prints inside.'

We opened the door wide; it opened into the building and immediately it was standing at its maximum we could see pieces of smashed glass on the floor. I led the way and halted in the entrance hall.

'So, Alan, what do you keep in here that would be worth stealing? There must be something.'

He thought for a while, his brow furrowed in

concentration and then he shook his head. 'Nothing, Nick. That's the daft part of all this – there's nothing in here to steal.'

'Bottles of lemonade?' I ventured. 'I've seen those being sold during matches – the kids love them, cherryade, lemonade, fizzy drinks of all kinds.'

'Oh, right, well, yes. We keep a few crates in the kitchen.'

'Let's have a look.'

Being club secretary, Alan kept meticulous records and in the case of the club's soft drinks, he maintained a running total on a list kept in a drawer in the kitchen. He found it, pulled it out, checked its figures against the stock in the cupboard and shook his head.

'All there, Nick. Not one bottle of pop missing.'

'So what else do you keep in here? Loose change? Tins of food, like soup? Tinned fruit? Biscuits? Tea in caddies . . . anything that can be used in the kitchen.'

'No loose change, no money at all. And we don't leave food on the premises in case it attracts vermin. The tea ladies bring it all in on a Saturday – well, it's every second Saturday really. We play one match at home and the next away, which is another reason we don't leave food here. Two weeks left untouched during a hot summer might not do it much good! I'll check though.'

He went through everything but could find no trace of theft. He also checked all the cupboards and lockers just in case something had been left behind, but found nothing. Whilst he was checking his inventory, I wandered around, chiefly to see if anyone was hiding on the premises but also to see if I could spot anything else of significance. I searched the floor, the cupboards, the lockers, the outdoor toilets – anywhere that I might find something or someone. I began to think the supposed break-in was nothing of the sort – it looked more like mere damage to the window even if it was close to the door lock.

I found myself back in the entrance hall with the door standing open and then I had a bright idea. I'd known detectives miss finding murderer's hats that hung behind a door because it opened against a wall and concealed them. People often left dressing-gowns in hotels because they were hanging on the back of the bathroom door . . . so I closed it. And there on the floor, tucked safely out of sight behind the door when standing open was a cricket ball. I picked it up. It was very new and in pristine condition, except for one or two slight cuts in the leather.

'Alan?' I called.

'Coming,' he said, as he emerged from the locker room of the away-team's quarters.

'A cricket ball!' I held it up. 'Down here, behind the door. One of the club's, you think?'

He took it from me and turned it over and over in his hand. 'No, it's not one of ours, Nick. Wrong make. Nice ball though, good condition. Fairly new, I'd say.'

'How about this for a theory,' I put to him. 'One of the village children, a keen cricketer, gets a cricket ball as a present. He comes down here for a knock around with a pal or two, then bang – one of them smashes it through the window, by chance very close to the door lock.'

'A child couldn't reach the pavilion with a strike, few of our adult players can hit a ball this far. We never get sixes in this part of the field.'

'And they wouldn't play close to the pavilion, would they? It's too rough, all that deep grass,' I said.

'Right, Nick. If they came down here for a knock around or a spot of practice, they'd use the main pitch – or one of the secondary pitches out there. They're all a long way from here.'

'So whoever hit this ball through that window must have hit it fair and square – a six by any standards, a man-sized stroke.' I smiled. 'And what's the first thing a chap does when he accidentally smashes a ball through a window?'

'Er, dunno, Nick.'

'He runs for it in case anyone has seen him! It's a natural instinct especially when playing cricket in the street, or in a car-park. Or even a deserted cricket field.'

'So you're saying this is not a break-in, just an accident with a cricket ball.'

'All the evidence points to it, Alan. And it's interesting the culprit didn't enter the pavilion to recover his ball. He could have done so very easily but he just made himself scarce. If he had come inside for his ball, we'd be no wiser about the cause of this modest drama. I think if he'd deliberately smashed the window with the ball, he'd have gone inside to retrieve it. So I think it was accidental.'

'Fair enough; I agree with that now we've had this chat. So what do I do with the ball? Can I keep it?'

'You know what I think? I think the club should keep it and have it mounted, then it could be donated to the player who gets a six by knocking a ball through one of the pavilion windows.'

'And if someone comes to claim it, before we get it mounted, I mean. What then?'

'Legally, it remains the property of the owner, but you could do some bargaining by saying he can have his ball back when he pays for the repair to the window. Or of course, he could donate the trophy.'

'It won't cost much to repair the window, one of our members is a glazier, he'll fix it for nowt.'

'Good, so I think you've got a new trophy to offer the players, to be held by the winner until someone else knocks a window out with a six. And I doubt if the owner will dare to claim his ball back.'

'Thanks, Nick. Sorry to have troubled you over this.'

'It's all part of the service, Alan. It could have been a crime but now I think not. I'll record it as 'No Crime' for our statistics, and put it down as accidental damage. Problem solved.'

For the record, we never did find out who had hit the cricket ball through the pavilion window, nor did we discover the origin or the owner of that ball. It was kept in the pavilion for display on a high shelf and although there was no legend to explain its presence, the story of the ball soon became part of the history of the cricket club. Within a few months, however, someone had painted a human eye on a square piece of wood and fastened it to the timber wall above the ball. Accompanying the realistic picture was a short sentence that said, 'Never take your eye off the ball.'

It is perhaps not surprising that the display became known as The Thackerston Eye Ball; it was eventually mounted on a base complete with the famous eye, and was awarded annually to the club's highest scoring batsman. If there was a draw, however, the one hitting the most boundaries was declared the winner.

Chapter 11

Bound By the Rules

One thing that had exercised my mind as a rural bobby in the months I had studied for my promotion exams was the need to saturate myself in the theory of criminal law and police procedure. Sometimes there was no time to look up a legal reference, or some obscure point of law; consequently I endeavoured to read and understand as much as possible so that I could carry out my duties in complete confidence. However, knowing the law was one thing – enforcing it was quite another and something I did learn was that there were times when one's senior officers did not tolerate constables who displayed greater knowledge than they themselves possessed. The need for diplomacy was never far away.

The statutes with which I had to be familiar included everything from the Firearms Act of 1937 to the Highways Acts of 1835 and 1959, by way of the laws of evidence, the

Judges' Rules and all the motoring legislation. There was also the Larceny Act, the Malicious Damage Act, liquor licensing rules, the variety of laws concerning children and young persons, a dozen or so statutes relating to dogs, a wide range of poaching legislation, how to deal with contagious diseases of animals, and thousands of other laws and regulations that police officers are supposed to know and enforce without fear or favour. And, above all that, there was Common Law with its own range of offences and powers.

In addition, there were the powers of arrest, the role of Director of Public Prosecutions, inquests, the progress of a case in a magistrates' court, the quarter sessions and assizes, and obscure laws like those relating to mechanical lawn mowers, animal boarding establishments, lights on trailers, rogues and vagabonds, pawnbrokers, billiards on Sundays, grey squirrels and stallions, riots and disorderly conduct, the registration of common lodging houses and, of course, police regulations. And much, much more.

When patrolling the beat, police officers do not have legal volumes with them for consultation in tricky situations – they must rely on their knowledge and common sense. At times they must make snap decisions in the knowledge that lawyers may later determine the matter in a court of law. It is one thing for a police officer to make a decision on the spur of the moment and quite another for teams of lawyers in the high court to decide whether his spontaneous action was lawful or not.

It all meant there was a lot to learn. One continuing problem was that the law and the way it was practised changed frequently and rapidly. Consequently, one major task was keeping myself up-to-date on almost a daily basis. I could do that by reading the Law Reports in *The Times* as well as learned articles in other legal periodicals. I discovered I could learn and understand some of the most complex of laws and procedures and that gave me confidence to carry out my multifarious duties.

So far as the practical aspects of law enforcement were concerned, my beat at Aidensfield seldom produced anything out of the ordinary. There had been very little to test my deeper understanding of the requirements of obscure laws because much of my work was very ordinary and almost boringly routine. I dealt with traffic accidents, road traffic laws and minor crimes, enforced the liquor licensing laws, the poaching legislation and the rules governing the transit and contagious diseases of animals. I made sure children and young persons behaved in a responsible manner and that people didn't allow their dogs to worry livestock, a particularly prevalent offence committed by visitors and tourists during the lambing season. It was amazing how many visitors allowed their dogs to run free in fields of sheep or cattle, or on the moors during the grouse breeding season. In other words, the policing of Aidensfield was really a very ordinary kind of policing, the benefit being that I worked mainly on my own without any close supervision. I had to make my own decisions for most of the time and it was my period as a country constable that would provide the testing ground should I ever be considered for promotion.

It was during my one of my legal swotting sessions that I

received a radio call from Inspector Breckon at Eltering. It was late evening and I was patrolling the area in my Mini-van, being responsible for the whole of Ashfordly section.

'Delta Alpha Two-Four receiving,' I responded.

'Report of arson on a car in the street at Ashfordly, Pottergate to be precise,' said Inspector Breckon.

'Arson of a car?' I queried.

'A Ford Prefect's on fire in Pottergate,' he said. 'The Fire Brigade is there now and they reckon it's arson. They've requested a police presence.

'There's no such crime, sir,' I responded.

'Don't come the old know-it-all with me, Rhea,' he said with more than a hint of humour in his voice. 'A car's on fire, the Fire Brigade reckons it's been set on fire deliberately, and in my book that's arson.'

It wasn't, but it was not my place at that moment to argue with my inspector, so I switched on my emergency blue light and drove as quickly as my little van would permit. I arrived within ten minutes or so as the Fire Brigade was smothering the smouldering wreckage with foam. It was in the street, well away from any garage or shed.

Always with burning cars, there is the risk of an exploding fuel tank, but it seemed the blaze on this old banger was now under control. A fire appliance was present with blue lights blazing and several fire officers operating hoses around the scene and directing foam on to the remains. As I arrived one of them approached me – I recognized Sub-Officer Charlie Sutton. In such situations, the police come under the direction of the senior fire officer present at the scene.

' 'Evening, Charlie,' I greeted him.

'Hi, Nick. There's nothing we can do for the car now, it's practically a burnt-out wreck, but we'll keep things under control. Fortunately the fuel tank hasn't blown up. No one's been hurt, it was empty when it was attacked. We called you because it's arson – somebody deliberately created this fire.'

'How?' was the obvious question.

'Combustible materials on the back seat, windows left open to create a through draught and enough stuff at the seat of the fire to ensure it burnt a long time once it got going. Time enough for the fabric of the car to ignite and blaze fiercely. We're not sure what the accelerant was – probably paraffin-soaked rags or paper, but there's no doubt it was arson.'

'You'll be arranging a forensic examination of the remains?'

'Sure, and we'll let you have a report. It's too early to be positive about the type of accelerant right now, but we've enough evidence to convince us it was deliberately set on fire.'

'So we need to find the arsonist!' I used his erroneous word!

'Well, you've a good start. Happily, the number plates have not been destroyed so you shouldn't have any trouble tracing the owner. He might know who did it – it smacks of a revenge attack.'

I did not air my knowledge about the legal impossibility of committing arson to a motor vehicle, but went along with the atmosphere of those important moments.

'Fair enough,' I said. 'I'll start enquiries right away and will arrange for our scenes of crime team to come and examine the remains and take the necessary photos.'

My early enquiries in the nearby houses established the Ford was owned by a young council worker called Alan Stevens. When I went to interview him, he shook his head and said he had no idea who might have destroyed his car. I felt he was not telling the truth – and later enquiries showed that Stevens was on the fringes of crime and this attack on his car bore all the hallmarks of revenge. As a matter of interest, I never discovered who might have caused the fire although, when in due course I learned that Stevens was heavily in debt, it occurred to me he had set his own car on fire as a means of claiming an insurance pay-out. The investigation into that possibility would be carried out by his insurance company, but with no fingerprints or witnesses, the true answer would be difficult to obtain. Setting goods and buildings on fire to claim insurance pay-outs was all too common.

When I settled down to compile my crime report relating to this incident, I caused both my sergeant and my inspector to reject my report on the grounds it was inaccurate. The sergeant had queried it with me, but when I had offered my explanation, he had agreed and had therefore passed my report to the inspector. Inspector Breckon rang me at home.

'PC Rhea, we've been through all this before. You have not recorded that burnt-out car crime as arson. You've shown it as malicious damage.'

'Yes, sir,' I said.

'It was a deliberate act of arson,' he said. 'The Fire Brigade has confirmed its early findings.'

'You can't have arson of a motor vehicle, sir.' I had to stand my corner yet again. 'As Common Law, arson was confined to the malicious burning of the house of another, including its outbuildings. That was the situation until the Malicious Damage Act of 1861 expanded the crime. It then included churches and places of divine worship, dwelling houses with persons therein, other houses, warehouses, shops, sheds etc, or any building used in farming, manufacturing or trade, railway stations, ports, dockyards, harbours, public buildings, agricultural crops, hay stacks and similar stacks of straw and other vegetable produce, mines of coal and other minerals, ships and vessels, whether complete or not, arsenals and magazines – and anything inside a building which was unlawfully and maliciously set on fire. But not cars, buses, lorries and motor bikes, sir. Or aircraft.'

'Why not?'

'Because they hadn't been invented in 1861 when that statute became law. The exception would be if the car or other machine were in a garage, and someone deliberately set fire to the garage. The whole crime would be considered arson.'

'And this car was in the street?'

'Yes, sir.'

'It's all a bit daft, isn't it?'

'From my researches, sir, I understand the law is under review. In the next few years, there could be a new statute dealing with all forms of criminal damage. It will include arson to modern things like cars and aircraft.'

'So if we can't call the crime arson, how is it we can refer to it as malicious damage to a motor car, if cars weren't invented in 1861?'

'There's a 'catch-all' section in the act, sir – section 51. It caters for damage to all kinds of property of a private or public nature that is not specifically catered for elsewhere in the act. But that's only for malicious damage, not arson.'

'Hmm,' he said. 'Well, I must congratulate you on this – I've learned something, so thanks, PC Rhea. You've stopped me making a fool of myself before the superintendent. But now I think I might have to put him right too. . . .'

Another practical use of my expanding knowledge was put into good effect in Aidensfield. It happened shortly after I arrived as the village constable, put it was something I had remembered from my days as a recruit in the training school. I might have already made reference to this tactic in an earlier diary – if so, forgive me! It concerned Aidensfield village inn, the Brewer's Arms, and its landlord, George Ward whose cousin, also called George Ward, ran the Hopbind Inn at nearby Elsinby.

Both Georges were excellent landlords and never gave me a moment's concern so far as the traditional drinking offences were concerned, i.e. drinking after hours, encouraging youngsters to congregate on the premises, or even selling intoxicants to drunken people. Nothing of that kind happened in these pubs because both were very well conducted.

The Brewer's Arms, which could accommodate about a dozen residents in its bedrooms, had once been a rather grand manor house and was therefore an extremely attractive building in its own spacious grounds. Built in local stone and dating to the sixteenth century, its interior was full of ancient oak beams and panelling. It boasted lots of interesting rooms with huge marble fireplaces, all of which were unspoiled by modernization. Its black oak staircase led upstairs from a hall that should have been full of knights in their armour and, like so many old houses, it also had a resident ghost. This was said to be a small boy who had died in mysterious circumstances years ago. He made his appearance on the staircase as if running from his bedroom. Sadly, I never saw him but it was claimed he had been seen by several residents.

The entrance to the Brewer's Arms was via its car-park that lay adjacent to the street. There was a large oak door that would have repelled any invader which opened into a small porch that in turn led into a large and airy inner room. This was not one of the bars of the inn, neither was it a lounge or dining room. This particular room had a fireplace and a stone floor but served as little more than a foyer or cloakroom where one might leave wet coats, dirty wellington boots or one's dog. Customers passed through it *en route* to all other parts of the old inn. On many occasions, I walked through the room, in uniform, to find a handful of young people in there. Most would be under eighteen. In time, they fixed a dartboard to one wall, found a card table and later persuaded George to install a pool table. That handsome if little used room thus became a type of rather modest youth club for Aidensfield. Not surprisingly, it attracted youngsters from Elsinby, Crampton and Maddleskirk, none of whose pubs had such a spare room. As I passed through upon my constabulary duties, the youngsters would look at me sheepishly, but I bade them good evening, or hello, or something perhaps a little more friendly, and did not chase them out. It was the latter act, in the very early stages of my duties in Aidensfield, that baffled them.

It was all to do with the myth that young people under eighteen years of age were not allowed in pubs. That was completely false – people under eighteen *were* allowed in pubs. They were even allowed in the bars of pubs during permitted hours if they were fourteen or over. A bar was defined as a place in licensed premises where there was both a sale *and* a consumption of intoxicants. The fact there may or may not be a counter is irrelevant – if intoxicants were sold and drunk in a room, then it qualified as a bar, and that is the place where so many restrictions lay.

If a room was used for drinking alcohol that had been purchased elsewhere on the premises, then that room would not qualify as a bar, e.g. a lounge or bedroom, so consequently many of the age restrictions would not apply. A child under fourteen should not be in a bar during licensing hours, unless passing through from one place to another, or if he or she was a resident in the hotel. In simple terms, therefore, youngsters were allowed in pubs – think of people on holiday with their family, or friends visiting the licensee.

However, there were restrictions. A person under

eighteen could not *buy* any intoxicants *anywhere in licensed premises*, but he or she could drink alcohol in the pub. It meant someone had to buy the drinks for those under eighteen and they could not consume their drinks in the bar. They must drink their alcohol elsewhere, say the lounge, dining room or even a bedroom. Furthermore, a person of sixteen could purchase beer, porter, cider or perry in a dining room for consumption with a meal.

In private premises, such as one's home or a friend's home, of course, there was no restriction on the ages at which a young person may drink alcohol, the exception being those under five years old who could only drink it for 'good reasons', this probably meaning for medicinal purposes. This might sound somewhat complicated but police officers had to be familiar with these rules if they were to understand and correctly enforce the licensing laws, and so it was that I applied those rules to the foyer of the Brewer's Arms in Aidensfield.

I knew that the law permitted youngsters under eighteen to be in that foyer because it was not a bar – there was no sale in there, merely the consumption of alcohol purchased elsewhere on the premises. Alcoholic drinks could only be bought in either of its two bars or in the dining room – of course, there was no restriction on the sale of soft drinks. However, alcohol could be drunk by under eighteens in that foyer, provided someone else had bought it for them. The landlord knew the rules because I had explained them carefully to him. I had also explained to the youngsters, placing a heavy emphasis on their responsible attitude whilst reminding them the landlord could exclude any troublesome person from his premises. I told the kids that if one of them was barred for any reason, his or her pals could still congregate here leaving him to endure a lonely life.

None of my regular supervisory officers questioned my apparent soft attitude with the village youngsters – after all, I had told them how I was making good use of the existing laws that in turn kept the youngsters off the street. In other words, I knew exactly where they were and what they were doing.

The only problem that arose was one evening when I was off duty and a visiting constable patrolling the whole of Eltering Sub-Division in a GP (General Purpose) car happened to find himself in Aidensfield one Friday evening around 9.30. He pulled into the car-park of the Brewer's Arms and, because the pub appeared to be busy, decided to pay a supervisory visit. What he found was apparently a village inn full of youngsters having a great time breaking the law and, without pausing to consider the wider implications, waded into the pub to seek out the landlord, George Ward. The constable's name was PC Gerald Morrison, a recent transferee from Middlesbrough Borough Force.

'Landlord!' he snapped. 'That entrance of yours is full of teenagers with drinks. It is my duty to report them all for consuming intoxicating liquor, or aiding and abetting the consumption of intoxicating liquor whilst under the age of eighteen. It is also my duty to report you for selling intoxicants to persons under age, contrary to the Licensing Act of 1964, section 169.'

'And who might you be?' asked George.

'PC Morrison of Eltering, on general patrol duties. Here is my warrant card if you are going to question my identity.' And he produced the card and showed it to George.

'Hmm,' said George. 'Wait a moment while I call the police.'

'I am the police!'

'I mean our village constable, PC Rhea.'

'Call him by all means,' snapped Morrison. 'He's obviously been neglecting his duty, or else these yobbos are taking advantage of his absence. He is off duty this evening, hence my visit. And a very timely and productive visit too, by the look of things. If he gets himself here, he can be another witness for me.'

And so George rang me. Although I was off duty, I decided I must attend this call for help, so I walked down, making sure I took my copy of *Moriarty's Police Law*. The youngsters cheered as I entered the fray, but Morrison decided to take me into a back room, away from public scrutiny.

'Look, Nick, I know you run a good beat, but I've just caught this lot boozing as if there's no tomorrow – the landlord must have sold the drinks.'

'Yes, Gerry, but no one's breaking any law.'

'We booked them for this sort of thing in Middlesbrough!'

'This is not Middlesbrough, Gerry. Look, those kids are not in a bar. . . .' And I set about yet another of my lectures on the liquor licensing laws. I was pleased I had brought *Moriarty* with me because it would back up my arguments.

171

Morrison took a lot of convincing, but in time he apologized to me and to George for blundering in like a two-ton elephant. Then I took him into the foyer where the youngsters were waiting in silence. I wanted him to talk to them.

'Look, folks,' he said, 'I'm sorry . . . I've just learned a lesson about our licensing laws, and another about dealing with youngsters. . . .'

The rest of his speech was drowned in cheers. I admired him for his fortitude because he took on the youngsters' very own darts champion – Andy Stewart – for a quick 301 up before resuming his patrol. And he beat him. Thereafter, I had no problems with the kids in the foyer of the Brewer's Arms – but I knew better than to challenge Andy Stewart to a darts match.

Chapter 12

Personal Boundaries

It is surprising how many people believe that minor wrongs committed personally against them are matters for the police to investigate. Certainly some wrongs are crimes or summary offences and therefore deserving of police attention, but others are beyond the scope of criminal law. However, they might be matters for the civil law. Such minor civil wrongs are known as torts, these being unlawful acts that might result in a civil claim for damages. However, there are many matters that cannot be accommodated within either the civil or criminal legal systems and in such cases, the first call for help is usually directed towards the police.

I had such a call from a Mrs Marigold Goodwin of Pine Tree Lodge, Crampton. She called shortly after 9.30 one Tuesday morning, fortunately catching me in my office just as I was preparing for my morning patrol. 'I have a complaint to make, Mr Rhea; perhaps you could call and discuss it with me?'

'Yes, of course. Is it urgent?'

'Well, it's not a matter of life or death but you will need to come fairly soon to see the evidence for yourself.'

'I can be there in about half an hour,' I said. 'I've a few matters to clear up in my office first. Can I ask the nature of the complaint?'

'It's about my neighbour, Mr Rhea. Mrs Ridgeway. I don't want to create any nastiness between us, so perhaps you could regard this as confidential. I can explain fully when you arrive – with the evidence in full view.'

And so on a fine, warm day in June, I drove to Crampton, one of the prettiest villages on my beat, and guided my van into the gravelled parking area of Mrs Goodwin's rather fine house. It stood on a hilltop site with open views to the north, these taking in the height and breadth of the North York Moors and almost the entire valley of the River Rye. Her view from the spacious garden at the front of the house stretched for several uninterrupted miles. My tyres crunched across the gravel as I pulled up outside the front door but, as is the custom in this region, I walked around a flagged path that led to the back door and rang the bell. She responded almost immediately. She was a stout, smart and well-spoken lady of indeterminate years, but probably in her fifties, and her husband was someone important in a local agricultural machinery business. He was at work. She led me into the kitchen where I was invited to have a coffee and some biscuits while she aired her complaint.

'It's that Mrs Ridgeway,' she said almost in a whisper.

'Your neighbour?'

'Yes, her house lies below ours. Our garden slopes down quite gently as you will see when we go outside, and the Ridgeways live at the bottom of our garden.'

'So what is your complaint?'

'She is obstructing our view, Mr Rhea. Almost every day . . . when I go into the garden, on a day such as this, I like to relax with a good book and a glass of white wine as I look across the dale towards the moors. It's such a glorious panorama, Mr Rhea. And she is spoiling it.'

'Deliberately? I mean, is she deliberately obstructing your view?'

'Well, no, I don't think so. That is why I want this conversation to be between just the two of us. I am sure she has no malicious intent, Mr Rhea, which makes things rather difficult. And she is a nice young woman who is really a very good neighbour. So I contacted you in the hope you can settle things amicably and give me some good advice.'

'So how does she obstruct your view?'

'With her washing, Mr Rhea. Every day. Nappies by the score. She has twins, you see, and every day she hangs rows of nappies on her line, right in the middle of my view. And on other days, there are sheets, pillow cases, children's clothes. . . .'

'But I thought your view was always clear?'

'From the house, yes. We're elevated here, but when I go to the bottom of the garden, to my special den, that's when I am faced with lines of washing fluttering and dancing in the breeze. I can see nothing but those nappies.'

'You'd better show me,' I offered, adding, 'but I ought to point out that this is probably nothing to do with the police. If there is no crime or offence, then it is not within the scope of my duty.'

'I thought there was some criminal offence of hanging out washing to the annoyance of other people? I'm sure I read it in a magazine recently.'

'There is a similar offence under the Town Police Clauses Act of 1847,' I told her. 'But that refers only to hanging clothes on lines strung across a street or public thoroughfare to the annoyance, danger or obstruction of residents and passers-by. And in any case, that old act is only active in certain towns − it doesn't include villages like Crampton, and it doesn't apply to wash lines on private property. Unfortunately, this is not a police matter, Mrs Goodwin.'

'Oh, dear, so what can I do?'

'To be honest, I doubt if you can do anything. There may be a remedy in civil law, but this is hardly the sort of action that would lead to damages being awarded.'

'But she leaves the washing out all day every day, Mr Rhea − just you come and have a look.'

After coffee we trekked to the bottom of her garden and sure enough, the view across the dale was totally obscured by two lines of nappies and other washing. Mrs Goodwin showed me her den, as she called it − a quiet part of the garden screened from her own house by a privet hedge, but equipped with a seat and a table offering what should be superb views across the dale.

'So, Mr Rhea, you can see my problem.'

'As I said, Mrs Goodwin, this is not a police matter and I doubt if you'd succeed through a civil claim of any kind. I think this is a good case for the Ways and Means Act.'

'I thought you said it wasn't a criminal offence?'

'It isn't. The Ways and Means Act is a saying we use in the force when we seek to resolve a matter by cunning or resourcefulness when no relevant statute applies.'

'Oh,' I don't think she understood the implications of what I was saying. 'What do you mean?'

'Do you sit down here every day?'

'To be honest, no, I don't. It's maybe twice or three times a week, depending upon the weather, of course.'

'If you were to light a very smoky bonfire down here before you came to sit and relax, provided the wind was in the right direction, then you might persuade her not to hang out her washing, or to leave it out . . . just an idea. Burning leaves make an almighty smoke, and burning paper makes bits fly all over the place.'

'Oh, but I couldn't, Mr Rhea.'

'Maybe a compromise. You will know when her washing is dry so that's the time to light your fire, just to persuade her or remind her to take it in. . . .'

She smiled. 'It might be worth a try, once in a while?'

'I think so.'

'Thank you, Mr Rhea.'

A few days later I received a phone call from Mrs Ridgeway. 'Excuse me ringing, Mr Rhea, but my neighbour Mrs Goodwin has taken to lighting bonfires while my washing is out. It leaves black marks all over the clothes. Isn't there a law against it?'

'Only if you light bonfires in the street,' I said. 'It's an old act called the Town Police Clauses Act of 1847. It doesn't affect bonfires on private premises.'

'So there's nothing I can do to stop her?'

'Perhaps the answer is not to leave your washing out all the time,' I suggested. 'Especially when she lights her bonfires.'

'Oh, I see,' she muttered, and rang off. I heard no more about the dispute although it reminded me of American Indians who used bonfires to send smoke signals. It seemed the messages contained in Mrs Goodwin's smoke signals were being received and understood.

Chapter 13

A Boundless Future

Mrs Hilda Henderson had been an invalid for many years, always lovingly cared for at home by her faithful husband, Jim. The couple had no children and no other relations – there was just Hilda and Jim. In her late seventies, Hilda never ventured out of the family home – she had a dread of appearing in public in a wheelchair and being considered someone incapable or even useless.

Certainly Hilda had her pride – if she couldn't walk, she wouldn't go – and she wouldn't be seen in her invalid and weakened state. As secretive as the mole, she liked to maintain her aura of mystery. Her physical condition meant she spent all her days in the seclusion of the house and garden, struggling to go about her own daily routine. She could dress herself, do some household chores and even cook a tasty meal so she was by no means inactive. However, no one was ever invited into the house and the

Hendersonts never socialized with other people – you never saw Jim in the pub, for example, or attending church, or going to any of the village events such as fairs, plant sales, garden parties and so forth. His only interest outside the house was his spacious and beautifully maintained garden. It supplied most of their fruit and vegetables. At the bottom, more than a hundred yards from the house, was a wild area with a seat nearby. It was here that Hilda liked to come to watch the butterflies and wild birds; she adored wild flowers too, and all things natural, especially trees and shrubs. For Hilda, the garden was her idea of heaven.

It was well know in Aidensfield that the Hendersons were devoted to one another and no one tried to interfere with their secretive way of life. They were left quite alone to conduct their lives as they wished. Perhaps the only sightings of Jim, now that he was retired, were when he pottered down to the shop for his groceries, or went to the post office for their pensions. If anyone asked after Hilda, he would say she was as well as could be expected, generally without adding any further comment.

I was dreadfully surprised and shocked, therefore, to receive an early morning phone call from Ray Collins, a near neighbour of the Hendersons.

'You'd better come quickly, Mr Rhea, I think Jim has killed Hilda.'

'Killed her? Are you sure?'

'As sure as I can be: he's buried her in the garden.'

'I'll come now,' I said.

Ray Collins worked for the Forestry Commission and when I arrived at his house, which overlooked the

Hendersons' garden, he led me upstairs to his bathroom.

'I opened my window this morning,' he said, 'to get some air into the bathroom after I'd had my morning bath, and saw Jim manoeuvring Hilda into a deep grave that he must have dug earlier. Overnight mebbe. She was wrapped in a shroud of sorts, but I could see her face. I am not making this up.'

'So where did all this happen?' To be honest, I did not believe what I was hearing.

'Down there, among those trees,' and he pointed them out to me. 'It took me a while to get dried and dressed, and then I dithered, not really knowing what to do, and by the time I'd done all that and gathered my wits, he'd finished. You can see the mound on the grave.'

'A mercy killing, you think?' I put to him.

'I don't know what to think, Mr Rhea. But they were very, very close and quite private. An odd couple, in many ways. We've never really got to know them, even if we do live next door.'

I took a deep breath. 'I'd better go around and have a word with Jim,' was all I could think of saying. A murder on my beat was not something I really relished – even if it was a mercy killing and we knew the killer. But it might lead to my very first arrest of a murderer, an ambition once held by many police officers. In such cases, a genuine mercy killing was usually reduced by the courts from murder to manslaughter, the culprit being let off with a correspondingly light penalty, although full murder enquiries would have to be made. And, of course, the culprit would inevitably be charged initially with murder.

181

The outcome depended upon the courts, not the police.

With very mixed feelings, therefore, I went around to the Hendersons' home and knocked on the door. Jim answered. He was a small, wiry man with a slight stoop and a head of fine grey hair.

'Morning, Jim,' I said. 'Can I come in?'

'Aye,' was all he said, walking ahead of me into the dark interior of his home. He led me into the dimly lit lounge with its dull carpet and brown leather settee with matching chairs. A small fire was burning in the grate, the flame barely visible among the tiny pile of coal. 'Sit down, Mr Rhea. So what can I do for you?'

'It's not easy for me to say this, Jim but I've had a report that you've been seen burying Hilda.'

'Aye,' he said. 'That's right.'

'Where?' I heard myself ask.

'Down t'garden, where she wanted,' he said.

'I had no idea she was dead, so when did she die?' I had no wish to accuse this old man of killing his wife; I hoped there might be another explanation.

'Four or five days back, Mr Rhea. She passed away one night. I got t'doctor in but it was too late. Dr McGee from Elsinby. Heart, he said. Her poor old heart had had enough so it just stopped. She was never in any pain, Mr Rhea. Nowt like that. She passed away beautifully.'

'The doctor certified the death?'

'Oh, aye, he gave me a form for t'registrar so I could go ahead wi' t'registration of t'death and then the burial. Then I got another form from t'registrar which said I could go ahead and have her buried . . . I've got all the paperwork here if you want to see it.'

Without waiting for my response, he went to a small bureau in the corner near the fireplace and pulled out a few documents that he gave to me. I read them quickly – they were as he had said, all genuine.

'I was surprised to learn she'd been buried in the garden.' I felt I had to clarify the matter.

'It's where she wanted, Mr Rhea, none of that churchyard stuff for our Hilda and she didn't want cremating. All she wanted was to be buried among her favourite trees and flowers in t'garden. So that's what I've done.'

'Didn't you have to get special permission to bury her in the garden?'

'Aye, planning permission from t'Council. They do checks to see if t'site is all right, not interfering with folks' drinking water or owt like that, and then they give permission. They did all that, Mr Rhea, it's all among them papers somewhere.'

Jim's action had certainly made me think. His documents were all in order and I had learned something about the law. It was possible to bury a human dead body almost anywhere, provided there were no complaints and the necessary authority was granted. Jim never asked why I had really called to see him but he did tell me it was also his wish to be buried beside Hilda down the garden. I must admit I wondered who would want to buy the house when both former residents were dead and buried there. And who would gain from the sale of their house if they had no family? I'm sure neither of the Hendersons cared about that.

I went back to Ray Collins and told him what I had learned. He merely shook his head. 'Well, I can't say I object,' he admitted. 'I've no qualms about a body being buried among those trees – it's no different from living next door to a churchyard, is it?'

'It's pleasant and quiet being near the dead centre of the village!' I cracked the old joke and then left. I still found it odd there were so few rules about the disposal of human remains although graves and graveyards were strictly protected by law.

One thing I did recall from my training school days was that it was impossible to steal a dead body because it had no owner. Maybe, if I received a report of the theft of a body, it would be another instance when the Ways and Means Act might prove useful. If there was no such crime as stealing a dead body, perhaps we could prosecute such a 'thief' for stealing the shroud or damaging the coffin, or stealing jewellery from the body, or for one of the many other offences of interfering with graves. For some unaccountable reason in the midst of all this, I was reminded of the words of the poet, Edmund Clerihew Bentley who wrote, 'There is a great deal to be said about being dead.'

Chapter 14

Bound by Duty and Service

The dull day in August did not inspire me to climb out of bed very early, particularly as I had been on duty until 1 a.m. that morning. But someone living on my beat had other ideas because it was barely eight o'clock when my telephone rang. Today, my tour of duty was scheduled to begin at 10 a.m. but all hopes of a lie-in evaporated at that moment. Mary and the children were already out of bed and having breakfast, preparing for an organized coach trip to Scarborough. I could not go because I was on duty and so I struggled downstairs to the office in my pyjamas feeling very weary. The prolonged ringing suggested an emergency of some kind. Mary and the children had not heard it – the kitchen was some way from the office and besides, there was quite a din as the excited children were preparing for their day out – the schools were on holiday.

'Aidensfield Police.'

'Is that the policeman?' asked a faint female voice.

'Yes, I'm PC Rhea. How can I help you?'

'It's Miss Harborough here, Mr Rhea. Cornelia Harborough. I hope you don't mind me ringing but it is important.'

'Of course I don't mind, that's why I am here. Is it an emergency of some kind? If so, I can arrange for another officer to attend – I am not on duty until ten o'clock.'

'It's not an emergency, PC Rhea, but something of great importance which I have found in my house. I would prefer you to attend, not some other officer unknown to me. After ten will be very convenient.'

I was acquainted with Miss Harborough from the past and knew where she lived. 'Good, so let's say half-past ten. So, in the meantime, can you give me some idea of what you want to discuss?'

'Not really, PC Rhea it is highly confidential and I wouldn't want other people to know about it. I know I can trust you – you were so kind to me over that sixpence I found, and about filling in my census return.'

'That was a long time ago, but I'll respect your wishes. I'll see you at ten-thirty.'

I remembered Miss Harborough well. She was one of the first people I encountered upon my arrival at Aidensfield several years ago. She must be in her late seventies or even early eighties and lived in a tumbledown wreck of a cottage which was filled with antique furniture, newspapers, rubbish and every kind of oddment one could imagine. Everything was piled on top of everything else – it was worse than Claude Jeremiah Greengrass's scrap-metal tip. I had no idea how she cared for herself and was unsure whether any relatives kept in touch with her. It was impossible to walk through any of her rooms – one had to clamber over the furniture or junk that filled every inch of space. Similarly, the garden was an unkempt patch of wilderness complete with briars, thistles and hawthorn bushes.

That first encounter was when she found sixpence in the road outside her house. Being a very honest person, she wanted to hand it in to the police as found property in the hope it would find its way to the rightful owner. That morning when I replaced my phone, I recalled my earlier efforts in trying to persuade her to keep the coin, saying I would enter it in our records and if the loser reported it to the police, then he or she would be directed to Miss Harborough to reclaim it. That was the most simple and logical procedure because she insisted on following the prevailing rules to the letter. For such a small sum of money, of course, most people would not bother reporting it and if the finder wished to salve his or her conscience, they would probably pop it into a charity collection box. But not Miss Harborough. She had insisted on handing it to me officially which in turn meant I had to go through all the recording procedures that affected an item of found property; I had to issue a receipt to her, record the finding of the sixpence in the Ashfordly Police Station log of found property, and then keep it in the Found Property cupboard for three months, unless it was claimed in the meantime. If it was not claimed, the police then had to write to Miss Harborough to say the property was unclaimed and that it now belonged to her – it would be restored to her by a constable against an official receipt. Quite a rigmarole for a mere sixpence!

At that time, Sergeant Blaketon had been far from pleased at this gross waste of time and administrative work for the sake of goods worth so little and he would not believe I had tried – and failed – to persuade the finder otherwise.

'Then you did not try hard enough, Rhea,' he had grumbled. 'What's happened to your powers of persuasion? All this administrative work for sixpence . . . what a waste of time. . . .'

Of course, when I took it back to her she didn't want it – she felt she had no right to someone else's sixpence, but she was agreeable to my suggestion of donating it to the Police Widows' and Orphans' Fund.

My second brush with her was when she wanted help to fill in her government census form. I said I would be happy to assist her but then she asked me to go to her house at midnight – because the form wanted to know who was resident in her house at midnight. In trying to duck out of that one, I explained I had to be in my own house at midnight so that all my family were correctly recorded and, happily, she saw the logic of my argument. But she persuaded a neighbouring farmer to attend her house at midnight so she could correctly fill in her form. He'd even put his name on her form, just to ensure everything was truthfully recorded.

It was with those past experiences in mind that I drove

to Miss Harborough's ramshackle home in Waindale to discuss her new problem. If her cottage had been well maintained, it would have been a delight. The cottage next door was also derelict and I wondered if she owned both. On the chilly summer morning, I parked outside the house and fought my way through the barrier of weeds and briars that obstructed the rough path through her garden. The front door was standing open but, so far as I could recall, it always stood open. I don't think it was possible to move it or to secure it; it was literally a piece of rotting wood hanging off rusty hinges. I rapped on the flimsy door and shouted and then Miss Harborough suddenly appeared, as if bobbing up from beneath her collection of junk.

'Ah, Mr Rhea, do come in,' she oozed.

I inched my way into the living-room to find a piece of floor space squashed between a table lying on its side, a sofa and a rolled up carpet.

'Just wait there, Mr Rhea, I shall bring it through for you to see.'

The stench was forbidding. It was a mixture of human body odours of the long-term unwashed kind, plus the scents that emanated from old, disused and damp furnishings like settees and armchairs. As I waited, I looked around the mass of rubbish, wondering how on earth she could assemble such a mountain of useless stuff and at the same time live among it. Then she returned, carrying a large object.

She placed it on an upright sideboard lurking among the junk and I saw it was a carved statue. It looked like wood –

oak in fact. It was exquisitely modelled and unpainted. It was evidently a male saint because there was a halo behind his head made from a wonderfully slender circle of oak. He was dressed in the habit of what looked like a Benedictine monk. With a bishop's crozier in one hand, he was standing on a rock and at his feet was squatting a large bird. The statue was about fifteen inches tall, I estimated, and built with a solid wide plinth. It was, I felt, a lovely piece of sculpture.

'There, Mr Rhea, what do you think of this?'

'It looks like a splendid piece of craftsmanship,' I said. 'A real work of art.'

'Yes, I agree but do you know what it is?'

'An oak carving of a saint by the look of things. It might even be St Cuthbert – that bird at his feet looks like an eider duck and they are often known as St Cuthbert's ducks. They breed in the Farne Islands where Cuthbert established himself and his monastery centuries ago. I think it might have been carved for a Catholic church or a Catholic lady chapel somewhere.'

'Well, I must say I did not know it might be St Cuthbert, but I recognized it as a well-executed statue of a saint. And that is the puzzle, PC Rhea. What is it doing in my house?'

'You found it here, didn't you? That's what you said when you called this morning.'

'Yes, I found it here as I told you, but that doesn't answer the question – what is it doing in my house? How did it get here?'

'Now that is something I can't answer off the cuff, as it were. Where did you find it?'

'I must admit, Mr Rhea, that I thought a thief must have stolen it from a church and hidden it in my house. The doors are always open and unlocked; anyone could have come in by night or day to hide it.'

'I think if a thief wanted to get rid of ill-gotten goods, he wouldn't bring them to your house, he'd throw them into a river or a dustbin or rubbish tip . . . so where exactly did you find it?'

'I will show you, Mr Rhea. Follow me.' I picked up the heavy statue and followed her.

She wove through her shoulder-high rubbish like a weasel threading its way through a thicket of brambles whilst I struggled to climb over a variety of furnishings or even, at times, to crawl on my hands and knees beneath tables which bore tons of clutter. But after moving through what seemed to be a labyrinth of rooms, we found ourselves in an outhouse near the back door. Linked to the house by a series of outbuildings, it was stone built and very dry inside, probably large enough to accommodate a child's pram and other assorted domestic oddments. But now it was full of newspapers piled high around the walls, all yellowed and tied in bundles with thick, hairy string – called Charlie Turner in these parts. Charlie Turner (or Charlie Tonner as it is pronounced locally) is used for a variety of agricultural and horticultural purposes chiefly because it is so strong and can survive almost any weather conditions.

'The statue was wedged between those two piles on the floor.' She pointed to the place. 'I almost didn't see it and then I saw the plinth sticking out a half-inch or so – this morning it was. I withdrew it to find this wonderful statue. Luckily, it was not crushed, but perhaps the piles of papers at either side and on top have helped to protect it.'

'It must have been firmly wedged in, with all that newspaper around it.' I could see the space it had occupied – over the years, the papers had welded themselves around the statue and now it was gone, the space remained. I took the statue and aimed it back into the vacant space, head first. I could see in the shape of the papers the outline of features like the statue's arms and head, so it was a comparatively simple matter to ease it back into position without damaging the halo. It must have been lying there for years and years.

'How did you get it out?' I asked. 'It must have been very tightly wedged in.'

'It was indeed, Mr Rhea. I prized it out using a garden hoe . . . stuck the blade into the space behind the plinth and levered it out gently – I put a cloth over the blade of the hoe, to reduce any damage.'

'You did very well indeed, there's not a sign of damage on it,' and I placed St Cuthbert on a smaller pile of papers near the doorway. 'So what do you want me to do?' I asked.

'Well, Mr Rhea, clearly it is not my property, so I thought I should report it. I have never seen it before in my life. I have no idea where it has come from or who put it there. Perhaps it was stolen and hidden, as I said. I think it is vital that you find the true owner. I don't want to be accused of stealing it.'

'I don't think that is likely! So how long have you lived here?' I asked.

'All my life, seventy-nine years, Mr Rhea.'

'And who lived here before your family?'

'My mother's family – then she married Dad, and they lived here. I was born here.'

'And before then?'

'My grandmother's family, on my mother's side, and my great grandmother's . . . the house has always belonged to us, Mr Rhea, it's our family home, descending through the female side for generations. The eldest daughter always got the house, it was somewhere to raise a family without worrying about rent or having to buy somewhere.'

'And a nice idea too. So let's see the dates on those piles of newspapers.'

With tons of papers piled on top, it would be difficult to part the compressed pages to find a date on the headings, but thanks to the gap left by the absent statue, I was able to thrust my fingers between the pages and find the dates.

The papers to the left of the statue's space were all from 1874 and those to the right of the space were 1901. It suggested to me that with the papers being stacked around the statue it had been there since at least 1901 or earlier – and in view of the history of the owners of the house, it must have belonged to her family.

'Miss Harborough,' I said, trying to sound official, 'all the indications suggest the statue belongs to you, having been passed down to you through the family. It is yours to do with as you please.'

'Oh, no, Mr Rhea, that cannot be true. I have never seen it before . . . all the years I have lived here, I have never seen the statue and no one in the family ever spoke about it. I cannot, in all honesty, make a claim that it is rightfully mine. That would be very dishonest of me.'

'Was something else ever stacked in front of it, as a matter of interest?'

'Yes, another pile of papers, but they got in the way when I tried to come in so I moved them. Only this morning in fact.'

'And that's when you discovered the statue?'

'Yes.'

'All the more reason for thinking it's a family heirloom. It must have been lying there for years, Miss Harborough, hidden from the world.'

'I understand what you are saying, but we can't overlook the fact it was *hidden*, Mr Rhea. Not stored, *hidden*! Very well hidden. Very neatly, too. Now why would anyone hide a statue among my newspapers?'

'I can't answer that, Miss Harborough but I do think it would have been placed there by a member of your family, probably seventy years ago or more. Who else could or would do such a thing? So, I am of the firm opinion that it belongs to you; it's a family heirloom and a very nice one too.'

'No, Mr Rhea, I cannot accept that, so I must stress I cannot claim it as mine. I am, therefore, handing it to you, for you to determine the rightful owner. Isn't that what you are supposed to do with found property that is handed to you?'

'We keep careful records, yes, and do our best to find an owner or to determine whether the property is actually stolen goods. In this case, I am convinced it belongs to the house; it has been here for decades and, as the current owner of the house, you have a strong claim of right to the statue. I cannot see anyone else lodging a claim for it.'

'I must disagree, PC Rhea. How on earth could I claim it as mine?'

'Could you not give it to a church, Miss Harborough? Or an art gallery, or museum?'

'I keep telling you it is not mine to give, PC Rhea,' she stated emphatically.

I could see we had reached an impasse and so I resorted to the old technique of dealing with it as if it was found property. 'I can accept it from you as reported found property, Miss Harborough, in which case I shall issue you with a receipt. It will remain in Ashfordly Police Station for three months, and if it is not claimed in that time, it becomes your property. That is the law. It means all the legal systems have been brought into play to determine ownership and you have done your utmost to determine that ownership, having taken all reasonable steps to trace the owner. You can't be charged with theft. Meanwhile, the police will carry out enquiries to try and determine who it belongs to and where it came from, probably with the help of the press.'

'And if, after the three months, it is not claimed, like that sixpence wasn't?'

'Then it will be returned to you, as your property.'

'But it can never be mine, Mr Rhea, never.'

'If you don't want it in three months' time, assuming it is not claimed, then you will be free to dispose of it as you desire.'

'But I can't dispose of something that is not mine, Mr Rhea. I do not want to be accused of theft, or receiving stolen goods, or whatever. That is what I keep telling you.'

I pulled out my pocket book, found a pad of property receipts in the back and wrote out one for the statue. I handed it to her.

'I'm leaving now, Miss Harborough, and I'll take St Cuthbert with me. I am sure we will find a suitable home for him.'

'Thank you, PC Rhea; you have eased my conscience at last. I did not like the responsibility of having it in my house.'

I was convinced the statue was a family heirloom so when leaving it in our Found Property store at Ashfordly Police Station I attached a note saying that Miss Harborough did not wish to have the statue returned to her and suggested it might find a good home in a church. After all, there was a church dedicated to St Cuthbert at Crayke in the North Riding of Yorkshire and I did not think the congregation would object to the statue of a Catholic saint/monk even if they were Anglicans. Or, of course, it could find a home in a Roman Catholic church among statues of the other famous northern saints. In my report, however, I did not say the statue had languished in Miss Harborough's home for seventy years or more. Quite simply, I said she had found it in an outbuilding – which sounded feasible.

I often wondered what would happen to the statue if no one came to claim it. It would have to be restored to Miss Harborough but I could visualize her refusing to have the lovely carving in her house. Perhaps my links with that statue were not yet over? I did not relish the idea of trying yet again to persuade her to keep it.

Chapter 15

From the Earth's Wide Bound

It is always exciting to make unexpected discoveries such as Miss Harborough's statue. Down the ages the law of England and Wales has catered for found relics and valuables unearthed during excavations or treasure hunts. In historic places such as York any excavation might reveal Roman artefacts, medieval coins or hidden treasure from almost any bygone age. Bones can be found too, whether they are human or animal, and such discoveries often turn up on ancient battlefields, or beneath the grounds of an old castle or manor house. Even when buildings were being demolished or improved, the removal of old stones can result in human bones being discovered in specially created cavities. Long before the era of Christianity, builders would incarcerate a living creature within the walls or foundations in the belief it would prolong the life of the building. Small animals were often the victims, but it was not unknown to wall up a young woman, a dreadful occurrence that produced long term ghost stories in the locality. Folklore accounts of such discoveries will often relate to ghost stories that ended when the remains were brought to light and given a Christian burial.

Because the area around Aidensfield was historic with features dating to the Stone Age and beyond, the discovery of human remains was not unusual. Bones of various kinds were discovered on the moors too, often working themselves to the surface over many generations although a lot of the discoveries were found to be sheep or deer. A visual examination of an ancient leg bone cannot always determine the species from which it came. Scientific examination is often necessary, even if the bones were unearthed on the site of a former Roman settlement. It should never be assumed the relics were from that area. Detailed examination of all such finds were made to establish that a modern murder had not been committed with the victim being buried in an old Roman graveyard. Once their age and likely source had been established, the bones were either re-interred or passed to a museum.

It was against this background that I found myself involved in such a discovery in Aidensfield. I was on duty one spring morning, on foot patrol around the village without any particular objective in mind. Such patrols were often productive because they encouraged people to stop the bobby for a leisurely unofficial chat, or even to pass on some useful information or observation.

I wandered around the green and made my way to St Aidan's Well, more out of curiosity than for any other purpose. The reason for my interest was that the water level appeared to be lower than normal and the well had never been known to dry up even during the most severe drought. The well was an important part of Aidensfield folklore. It was said that when St Aidan was passing through the village before he died in AD 626, he stuck his staff into the earth of a dry field at this point and water appeared as if by a miracle. The water was pure and fresh and was found to cure the ailments of both man and beast. Such pure water did not cure ailments – quite simply it did not cause them as did other polluted water. It was from that time that the village became known as Aidensfield, with a slight variation of spelling Aiden/Aidan. Some of its earlier names included Avensfeld or Adenesfelt. It had been the custom to use the well's water to fill the flower vases and piscinas in St Aidan's Catholic church, a stout stone structure built in 1456.

Over the years, the well, which originally was little more than a puddle on the green, was encased within a fine stone trough and strong surround, with the water always flowing but never flooding. There seemed to be a natural overflow system that took away any surplus. Not surprisingly the well became known as the Aidensfield Wishing Well. Certainly, people of the past regarded it as a holy well, saying prayers before it and decorating it with flowers, and it is not difficult to make a prayer seem like a wish. Maidens would come to the well in an attempt to determine the name of their future husbands, throwing in coins in the hope it would make any difference. Businessmen too would toss money into the waters in the hope their enterprises would flourish, some of whom undoubtedly uttered prayers to St Aidan for help and guidance.

As I stood before the well that morning, I was sure the flow had reduced somewhat and found it puzzling. Then I heard a voice; someone was heading towards me. It was Rudolph Burley, chairman of the parish council, a heavy man who lived up to his name, who earned his living as an auctioneer.

'A problem, Nick?' he asked, having seen my study of the water.

'Dunno, Rudolph. I was thinking the flow isn't as good as it has been.'

'Well, it should be OK; we've had plenty of rain and no sign of a drought. But you could be right, it does look a bit weak.'

'I've never seen it look like this,' I persisted. 'It's almost as if there's an obstruction somewhere along the inlet.'

'That's never happened before,' he told me. 'We've always had a good strong flow. As it comes down from the moors, there's a big catchment area. For a small outlet, it's got a mighty good watershed.'

'I thought it welled up from under this green?' I ventured.

'That's the legend, Nick. When Aidan stuck his staff into this ground, I reckon he knew there was an underground stream just below the surface, coming down from the moor behind us. He punctured the surface and up sprang the water, as if by a miracle. Since then, Nick, successive parish councils have taken steps to channel the water to this point, there's underground pipes now and an overflow system to take the surplus into the beck. If that hadn't been done, the water could have flowed anywhere, given the fact the earth shifts from time to time. We've plans of the pipes somewhere in the council files, so if you think the incoming flow is weak, then there might be a blockage somewhere.'

'Is there any way of checking where the blockage might be? It's not too serious yet but debris can gather around a small dam. If that happens, it could burst out somewhere else and divert the flow away from here.'

'And if that happens, bang goes our precious St Aidan's Well! We can't allow that so leave it with me, Nick. I'll have words with Stan Calvert if I can drag him away from his cricketing duties, he knows all the moorland water courses as well as he knows the veins on the back of his hand.'

And so I left the green to continue my leisurely patrol around Aidensfield, popping into the shop and garage for a chat and generally making my presence known. But nothing else was reported to me that day.

Over the next few days, I thought no more about the fate of Aidensfield's St Aidan's Well although whenever I was in its vicinity, I peeped into the trough to see how the flow was progressing. It barely seemed to change but it was far below normal.

It was a chance conversation with Jim Napier, the postman, who noticed my interest one morning and told me, 'They're working up there, Nick, somewhere on Raven Rigg. They reckon Stan's found the blockage and its spouting water out of a hillside to run away into one of the moorland becks.'

'Good, then let's hope they shift the problem and our famous well returns to normal.'

'Aye, we mustn't let it get neglected, Nick. It can easy happen, overlooking summat like this until it's too late. I'm glad our council's got involved with this.'

Later that day, I had several calls to make at remote moorland farms where I was undertaking my quarterly check of livestock records and when I was leaving Moorcock Edge, my radio crackled into life. I eased into the roadside to answer it.

'Delta Alpha Two Four receiving, go ahead.'

'Alf Ventress here, Nick. What's your location?'

'Just leaving Moorcock Edge above Aidensfield,' I told him.

'Can you go to Mill Wood Scar, speak to a Mr Calvert? Apparently he's found a buried body and is sure it's human. They think it's very old.'

'When was this, Alf?'

'Not long ago, half an hour mebbe. They'll suspend operations until you arrive; they're doing something to a moorland watercourse up there.'

'Have any other services been called?'

'Not yet, Nick. We need your assessment first. There's no point in calling an ambulance, it's a dead body and they won't turn out for that. And if it's old animal bones, as some of these discoveries often are, then we don't need Scenes of Crime and the rest of the cavalry. So go and have a look and report back here as soon as you can.'

It took me about twenty minutes to cover the rough

tracks that led across the open moors towards Mill Wood Scar and, as I brought my Mini-van to a halt, I could see the small knot of people waiting anxiously. I got out and walked towards them feeling somewhat apprehensive. A body on the moors? It could be murder . . . or a wandering tramp who had died alone, or a suicide. . . .

'Now, Stan,' I said, as he came towards me.

'Now, Nick. Rum do if you ask me.'

'So what's the story?'

'Not a lot to tell, really. We're digging here because it's where the water's emerging from underground instead of flowing downhill to the Aidensfield Well. We reckoned the pipeline is blocked hereabouts, causing the back-up of water and an overspill whilst reducing the flow in the village.'

'Right, got you so far.'

'Well' – Stan drew a deep breath – 'I was wielding my pick axe and it sprang off a rock under the peat and struck summat below the surface, just below, only a few inches. I shifted the turf with a spade and found a human skull, with my pick axe sticking in it.'

'Are you sure?'

'Aye, well, it wasn't a load of mushrooms or a rabbit, Nick.'

'No, I mean are you sure it's a human skull? Not a dead sheep perhaps?'

'It's human, Nick, make no mistake about that. I know a sheep's skull when I see one.'

'Right, you'd better show me. So have you touched anything?'

'No, I know better than that. I left everything just as it was.'

He led me the hundred yards or so to the scene. The water was gushing out of the peat and flowing heavily down the moorland slope, although some of it was still entering the pipe that would carry it to Aidensfield. But there, among the deep brown peat and water, was a skull with a pick axe embedded in it. It was human, I was fairly sure about that, but its discolouring and lack of any flesh suggested it was very ancient. I wondered where the rest of the skeleton was.

I stooped for a close look but took care not to touch anything just in case we were looking at a murder victim. If this was part of a complete skeleton, then the rest of it would be under the undisturbed patch of peat close to the water outlet.

'I'll have to call in our experts, Stan. Scenes of Crime, forensic pathologist and probably an archaeologist or expert on ancient remains. And if I know our CID, they'll bring the Task Force to dig up the rest of this piece of moorland, to seek any more remains. My betting is that it's a very ancient skeleton; these moors are covered with Stone Age tombs, ancient howes and burial sites.'

'So our job's called off then?'

'For the time being, yes.'

'So can I remove my pick axe?'

'Sorry, not yet. And I can't let you go either. We'll all have to wait until the experts arrive to get our stories. We don't need to stand right here, we can move away. I doubt if we're going to get crowds of onlookers.'

'So will this be sealed off with that yellow tape and will one of those little tents appear, where the scientists work away from cameras and things?'

'That's the way it is, Stan. It will be treated as a crime scene until we get the all-clear.'

'So what about the water running out of St Aidan's Well? Will it be contaminated? I can't say I would want to drink water that's been flowing around a dead body, even if it has been running for centuries. And don't they still use it for the flowers in the Catholic Church?'

'I think it might be wise for the council to seal off the well until this has all been sorted out, Stan.'

'Right, I'll see to that. It's upset me, you know, hitting that skull with my pick axe. It was like cracking an egg. Sad to think it was human.'

'I am sure we'll determine the skull is very ancient indeed, Stan, with no sign of life for hundreds of years. But it's out of our hands now. All we can do is wait until the experts have completed their examination of the scene and the remains.'

Within the hour, the experts began to arrive in their vehicles and set about examining the scene. My task was to take a written statement from Stan and his helpers as a forensic pathologist took a close look at the skull and archaeologists examined the upturned turf and remains of the water course. Everything was done meticulously with all unexplained objects being listed and their locations marked.

Then the signal was given for the six Task Force members to begin digging up the area in which the skull had been discovered. It didn't take them long to find a rough stone coffin containing bones – there were ribs, arms and legs all laid out neatly in the ancient stone container.

'A child,' one of the archaeologists commented. 'Buried here thousands of years ago. A child of important parents, judging by the coffin . . . we've found similar burials on these moors. I can safely say this is not a murder investigation, PC Rhea, I'd guess we're thinking of a death that occurred in an ancient civilization.'

'So what happens to the remains?' I asked.

'You need to inform the coroner just to fulfil the legal requirements, but I think he will allow them to be taken to a museum.'

'Right,' I said. 'And the next question, which I am sure will be raised by the villagers – is it safe to drink water from St Aidan's Well?'

'I don't think the water was flowing through the coffin, otherwise some of the bones would have been swept away, so the bones have come to light only as a result of earthworks close to the water supply. I'd say the water was safe – after all, it's been drunk and used for flowers for more than thirteen hundred years.'

Once the fuss on the moors had died down, and the newspapers had published their version of events, I returned to inspect the well in the village. The water was flowing heavily, just as it had done in the past but now it was a dark peat-coloured brown.

I thought it might clear within a few days, but I did hear one or two residents say, 'I wouldn't drink that stuff now' even though people had been drinking it and making good use of it for hundreds of years.

Nonetheless, some of the older characters thought it might be useful in their gardens and some wise-cracker christened the skeleton, 'Aidensfield Pete'.

Chapter 16

Breaking the Bounds

One thing I learned during my early years in Aidensfield was that many rural people seldom ventured far from their home village or small town, and rarely took holidays. The reason could have been due to lack of money for such inessential activities, holidays and days-out being regarded as luxuries. There was also the fact that a working life among animals required full-time care of all the creatures, and that included cats and dogs. Many of the people in and around Aidensfield worked on the land either as farmers or farm workers and they did not go away even for a weekend, knowing they could not leave their valuable livestock unattended. In short, most farmers and livestock owners never took a holiday that was longer than a single day. Their 'holiday' could be a visit to an agricultural show, cattle mart or farm sale, the intention always being to return home in time for milking, feeding-up and mucking-out.

The Corby family to whom I referred earlier was one exception to that generalization, although the local people who were not farmers sometimes travelled around Britain. Usually in the course of business rather than for leisure. The era of cheap travel overseas and regular Continental holidays was on the horizon but had not then reached peak popularity. Nonetheless, overseas travel by aircraft rather than ship had become almost within the reach of everyone. However, neither my parents nor those of my wife ever spent a holiday overseas and certainly never flew in a commercial aircraft (I think both dads might have flown in military aeroplanes). Indeed, neither my wife nor I experienced our first flights to a holiday destination until 1984 when we celebrated our silver wedding.

Adventurous people were beginning to think about flying off to places like Spain or Italy, and certainly those fortunate enough to own cars began to explore the British Isles. I recall several who returned from a week's holiday proudly proclaiming they had driven considerably more than a thousand miles, ostensibly to visit exciting places, but in fact spending most of their time on the road. They seemed to relish the freedom it offered – far easier than walking or travelling on horseback. It was rather like those Americans who 'do' Europe in a week. Such achievements represented a new, exciting form of personal freedom.

It was the rise of car ownership among ordinary people that changed popular seaside resorts around the country, including Scarborough and Whitby; hitherto, visitors would travel by train or coach to spend a week or more in such places, but ownership of a car meant they could travel there and back in a single day. The birth of the day tripper had begun and with it an entirely new form of leisure with the inevitable commercial benefits.

When I bought my first private car, a 1936 Austin 10, I began to explore the North York Moors and Yorkshire Dales with my girlfriend who eventually became my wife. In the early 1960s I can remember arriving at Osmotherley, a village on the western edge of the North York Moors, and then parking in the village to enjoy a stroll to the interesting old church and the Lady Chapel on the hills above. An old man sitting on a seat in the centre of the village hailed me to ask if he could help to direct me anywhere but I thanked him and said I knew my away around.

'Aye,' he said. 'And Ah know my way around these parts.'

'You've lived here a long time?' I asked.

'All me life,' he smiled. 'And Ah's ninety-two now.'

'You don't look it.' I trotted out the familiar compliment.

'Farmed 'ere since Ah was a lad, and me father before me and his father before that.'

'You must know the area very well,' I said. 'Have you travelled far in that time?'

'Aye,' he said. 'Ah once went to Northallerton, an' it was market day.'

'Is that all?' I had to ask.

'Aye, that's it, lad.'

Northallerton is a market town a mere eight miles away.

Another local tale that bears repeating concerns an elderly lady who had never been out of her dales village.

Anxious to show off his new girl friend, her grandson arrived one day with his car and said he would take her out for a drive. They drove up Wensleydale and then high across the magnificent route known as the Buttertubs Pass that separates it from Swaledale. The views from the summit of that pass are quite incredible with visibility stretching some fifty miles or more. At the summit, the grandson parked so that his grandmother could take in the view. She sat in stunned silence for a while and then said, 'I never knew the world was such a big place.'

One oft-repeated tale from the North York Moors concerns a farmer called Herbert Harland who owned a considerable acreage of land in the dale below his farmhouse. From his windows he could look over his land and, with the aid of binoculars, check the welfare of his livestock and the progress of his crops. One morning Herbert was standing at the front gate of his house peering into the northern part of the dale with his binoculars when a car halted nearby. A tall, wide gentleman with an equally tall, wide hat and brightly patterned jacket strode towards him. In a broad and loud Texan accent, the man asked for guidance to Castle Howard and then onwards to Scarborough. The farmer was happy to oblige by giving very precise directions.

'Is this your spread?' asked the Texan before leaving.

'Aye,' said Herbert, pointing into the dale below. 'My land follows yon hedge to the south, across the beck and through that wood, then over to the right, through that hayfield and back along the ridge to this spot. Three hundred acres.'

'Well,' said the Texan, 'when I go out on a morning, I take my jeep and drive east for an hour and a half, then turn south and drive for two more hours and head west for another three hours before turning and heading back to the ranch, that's another two hours. That's a whole working day to do a complete tour of my estate.'

'Aye,' said Herbert, not impressed. 'I've a car like that.'

It was Herbert who once provided a useful idea to me. One chilly January morning I called at his farm for the usual quarterly check of his livestock registers and noticed his old car parked on top of the midden.

For those who don't know about middens, they are large piles of cow, pig, horse and hen muck cleared from buildings on a daily basis. Well mixed with forks and shovels, the stuff is kept in the farmyard until eventually spread upon the fields as manure. A midden could therefore be four or five feet high and the length of a cricket pitch. It was well packed due to the weight of each new heavy layer of fresh deposits and some parts were often very firm on top where thick older layers had baked in the sun. Even so, a lot of smelly fluid flowed from them and was usually hosed down the drains. More often than not, the midden was directly outside the kitchen door, but the powerful stench did not appear to concern the human occupants. A midden, therefore, was simply a massive dung heap, a good source of free fertilizer.

It was on top of that midden, therefore, that I spotted Herbert's old car and the wheelmarks leading up to the top of the pile clearly showed this was a regular trip. The stuff was sufficiently packed by the weight of the car to provide both a solid path and an equally solid parking place.

'I see your car's parked on the midden.' Out of sheer curiosity I raised the matter as we enjoyed our coffee and cake.

'Aye,' he said, grinning. 'There's no better spot for a car in winter. It's warm underneath, Nick, because the midden chucks out a great lot of heat that's wasted otherwise. It makes my car start first time, even on the coldest day in winter. Useful things, middens. I've never known why garages don't have underfloor heating. You'd think somebody would invent it, eh?'

'Perhaps they will,' I said, not raising the question of what the interior of his car smelled like. Even though Herbert had a car, his trips out were mainly for farming business or to convey his wife and her collected eggs into market for sale. The idea of using it to have a day in Scarborough or the Lake District never occurred to either of them.

Sixty-five year old Jake Thetford farmed at Thackerston and he was one of the old-fashioned types who did not believe in holidays or outings. He had been brought up as a lad not to waste good money on such things and his entire life had consisted of constant hard work with very little reward. His married life was the same. His wife, Annie, was a good, hard-working woman whose background was similar to that of her husband, but when both reached pensionable age, they had money to spare. The state gave them a weekly income for doing nothing and for Annie, that was heaven. After all, they had spent a lifetime working hard and paying their taxes, so the pension money had been earned.

Jake, however, did not wish to be seen dependent upon charity, as he put it, and stubbornly refused to retire.

Knowing that very old age was rapidly approaching and that they had never had a holiday, or travelled anywhere except to Malton Mart and sometimes York, Annie decided they would take time off and have their first holiday. She'd always fancied going to Scotland and so, one Sunday morning after Jake had been to chapel and had returned in a moderately calm mood, she broke the news.

'Scotland?' he shouted. 'Who wants to go to Scotland? And what for?'

'For a break, to see the lochs and mountains; to see something of a different country. . . .'

'Ah can't see t'point o' that, our Annie. Ah'm not going anywhere!' said Jake.

'Yes you are,' she countered. 'It's all fixed. Ah've arranged for Ernie Furnell to come and see to t'farm while we're away, and Ah've booked us into a bed-and-breakfast house near Selkirk, that's for our first night. Then we can go into the Highlands and explore, find other spots to stay. . . .'

'Ah've never heard owt so daft in all my life,' he grunted.

'It's our wedding anniversary,' she reminded him. 'You always said we would go away on our ruby wedding. It was a promise, Jake. So if you don't go, I'll go on my own.'

'On your own?'

'Ah can allus go by trains and buses.'

'But a woman in a foreign country? No wife of mine is going to do such a thing, mark my words.'

'So we'll go, then?'

'Ah can't afford it.'

'Ah've saved up from the egg money.'

'Ah've nowt to wear.'

'There's that jacket and trousers you bought for your brother's celebration at work, when he got that Fire Service medal, and then there's that suit you got for your dad's funeral, and umpteen shirts and socks . . . you've plenty to wear.'

Jake knew he was beaten and so it was they packed their rather ancient Ford and headed north to the border country. He drove quietly and well, noting the state of fields, farmhouses and outbuildings on the way criticizing most of them for a lack of maintenance and bad crop management. They found the boarding-house on the outskirts of Selkirk, then Jake had a mighty shock.

'How much?' he barked at the landlady, as she outlined her terms.

'Nineteen shillings and sixpence, Mr Thetford, and that includes bed, breakfast and an evening meal.'

'But that's nearly a pound!' he shouted. 'There's no way Ah'm going to pay that sort of money just for a bed overnight and summat to eat.'

The offer of a minor reduction to eighteen shillings and ninepence did not appease him and so he said, 'Come on our Annie, we'll find somewhere cheaper.'

But they didn't. They tried six bed-and-breakfast establishments all of which cost around the same as their first offer and so he said, 'Annie, this is no good, no good at all. Ah can't think what got into you, wanting to come to such an expensive spot as Scotland. We'll sleep in t'car tonight;, that'll save us summat, then tomorrow we can get somewhere cheaper.'

Despite Annie's heartfelt protests, he found a lonely route that led deep into a dark, dense forest. In pitch darkness, he pulled up in the forest, parked and said, 'Right, there's no traffic here, let's get our pyjamas on.'

Nervously in the darkness, Annie obeyed, thinking that perhaps tomorrow would be better. They tried in vain to get comfortable in the back seat as the windows misted over in the cool air of that Scottish night. The cold began to have its effect, and they realized they could not stretch their legs and get comfortable wrapped in the horse blankets they always carried for emergencies. The front seats were in the way.

'Then I'll take 'em out,' announced Jake.

He left the car, opened the tool box in the boot and began to remove the bolts that secured both front seats.

He was accustomed to such work, doing most of his own repairs to his ageing collection of agricultural machinery and in time, he had both seats completely out. He stood them outside on the verge beside the car.

'Right,' he said. 'That's it. Now we can get some sleep.'

And so they settled down yet again, the car windows steaming up as the tough and tired couple sank into a very disturbed and uncomfortable sleep. Early next morning they were awoken by someone banging on their car roof.

Jake, unaccustomed to people and alarm clocks rousing him from his slumbers, took a while to gather his wits and to appreciate his whereabouts but he opened his window and asked, 'What's up?'

A strong Scots accent responded. 'You'll have to move your car, mister, you're parked on the road through the forest and we want to get to work.'

'Road, this is no road.'

'It's a forest route, sir, and you are obstructing it. You will have to move your car. You are trespassing too; this is private land. There is a queue of forestry vehicles waiting to get through.'

Still in his pyjamas, Jake struggled from the uncomfortable vehicle and stood facing his visitor. 'Aye, right, but Ah'll need to re-fit the front seats, Ah can't move it without the front seats where they should be. . . .'

'What front seats?'

'Well, they were there last night, Ah took them out myself.'

'They're not there now, sir, so we'll have to push your car off the road and then maybe you can find your seats.'

I was told this story by a Scottish policeman friend, and although Jake managed to secure some seats from a scrap yard to replace those that had been stolen, he vowed never to return to Scotland and never to take another holiday.

So far as long distance travel was concerned, I had occasion to visit Mrs Sally Rutland who lived in Pound Cottage, Aidensfield. A widow of several years, she lived alone in a very neat little house and always managed to produce a tidy garden full of flowers. Most of her time was spent tending her plants and her small greenhouse.

One afternoon I popped into the Aidensfield Stores to buy some stamps and postcards when the owner, Jack Carver, hailed me.

'Nick,' he said, 'I've found this in the shop.'

From a drawer, he produced a silver necklace bearing a small dark green stone held in a clasp. As he handed it to me, I could see the rather delicate catch was broken, the supposition being that it had fallen from the owner's neck without her realizing.

'Is it valuable, do you think?'

'Dunno,' was his honest answer. 'That jewel might be glass or some common stone. Silver chains aren't very expensive, are they?'

'So when did you find it?'

'This morning when I was sweeping up some spilt flour. It was under the edge of a shelf, kicked there perhaps, but I've no idea how long it's been there.'

'Any idea who it might belong to?'

'Sorry, Nick, no idea. We do get visitors in so it might not belong to one of my regular customers.'

'You've asked around?'

'No,' he shook his head. 'If it is expensive, I wouldn't want someone claiming it if they weren't the rightful owner. That's why I'm telling you. I know you've got procedures for dealing with such things.'

'Yes, we have. I can check our lost property register at Ashfordly Police Station to see if anyone's reported it missing, but other than that, it's a case of waiting until someone reports it lost.'

'Will you retain it, Jack? In case the loser comes here looking for it? If you do, then I'll mark it in our records. But meanwhile, I will check our lost property lists and, of course, if it's not claimed in three months, it becomes yours.'

'Oh, I don't want it, Nick. I have no right to it.'

'It will save a lot of time, effort and paperwork if you keep it,' I said. 'If anyone has reported it lost, I'll send them here. All you have to do is get the person to describe it so you are sure she's the right person to hand it over to – as you say, don't advertise it as found, otherwise you could attract a false claimant.'

Not all that happily, he agreed and so I went home and rang the office at Ashfordly Police Station. Alf Ventress answered.

'Alf,' I began, 'a found property check please. I've got a local man reported finding a nice silver necklace. I've no reports of a lost one so can you check the lost property register?'

'One minute, Nick.'

I heard him plonk the handset on the office counter and could then hear him flicking through the pages of the thick register.

'Yes, Nick. There's one here, a silver necklace with a green stone, lost a week ago. Not worth a great lot but it has some sentimental value; it was an anniversary present from the loser's late husband.'

'Where was it lost?'

'She didn't know, but thought it might have been in Ashfordly when she was shopping here. It's the only one of that description we've got reported.'

I explained what had happened and after hearing my account, Alf said, 'It sounds like the same one, Nick. The loser wasn't sure where she'd lost it, and she does come from Aidensfield, name of Sally Rutland. She could have lost it in your local shop. I told her if it was found in Aidensfield, we could get to know anyway. I explained how our system works.'

'Thanks, Alf. I'll go and see her straight away.'

Mrs Rutland, whom I knew quite well, answered my knock and invited me in. She led me into her small kitchen with its fire blazing in the grate and a kettle singing on the hob. She did not ask my purpose and I saw that her kitchen table was covered with travel brochures and airline leaflets.

'Mr Rhea, it's so nice to see you. Would you like a cup of tea, and then you can tell me why you are here? I am about to make a pot. Sit down in that chair.'

I settled down as she busied herself with tea and biscuits, and noticed some of the brochures were from Australia and others from New Zealand. I wondered if she was planning a holiday or perhaps going to visit relations.

She pulled a small occasional table towards me and placed my cup and plate of biscuits before me, then settled in the armchair opposite.

'So, Mr Rhea, what brings you here? This is quite a surprise.'

I explained about the necklace and how Jack had found it whilst sweeping out his shop. As I spoke, I could see tears of happiness welling up in her eyes. I described it in fairly close detail and she nodded.

'It sounds like mine, Mr Rhea. I was so sure I'd lost it in Ashfordly.'

'Jack has kept it in case the loser calls in. If you go and see him, he'll hand it back to you. In fact, I could go with you, just to keep the record straight. The clasp is broken, by the way but it can be repaired, can't it?'

'Yes, I can have it done in Ashfordly.'

'Then I am so pleased he found it. I suppose you are lucky, it could have been swept up and lost for ever.'

'It's odd, Mr Rhea, so odd that you should come just at this very time. Poor Dan, he was never very well you know. He bought me that necklace for our silver wedding. We had planned to go on holiday, over to Greece; he'd always wanted to experience the Greek way of life and see all those wonderful ancient ruins, but he died before we could make the arrangements. But thanks to a very honest shopkeeper, I still have my necklace and memories. . . .'

'Are you going on holiday soon?' I gestured towards the pile of brochures.

'No,' she said. 'I never go anywhere in person, but I can dream, Mr Rhea. I can dream of Dan and me going to Australia, New Zealand, Canada, South Africa, France, Greece, Italy. . . . I get the brochures, you see. Now my necklace has been found, I shall imagine I am on a trip to Australia. Then I find out all about the country and the area I would like to visit, and I check the flight times so I know exactly when the plane is taking off and where from, and what time it arrives. When an aeroplane comes over Aidensfield, I imagine it going to my destination and carrying me and Dan. It's all so real to me. Last month, before I lost my necklace, we went to Norway and Sweden . . . it was a lovely trip.'

'What a wonderful idea.' I smiled at her in her loneliness. 'I am sure Dan is with you all the time.'

'He is, I think his spirit is in this necklace. I had the

necklace then, Mr Rhea, I never go anywhere without it and was thinking I might not get anywhere until it was found. So you see, you have opened up lots more exciting places for Dan and me to visit. After Australia, I think it will be New Zealand and Dan always said he would like to visit the Pyramids and the Great Wall of China.'

'It sounds marvellous,' I had to say.

'Yes it is, and now I have a lot of planning to do, Mr Rhea. Dan and I hope to travel the world before we are too old.'

'But you must get the necklace repaired first.' I realized I was speaking as if she was going to go on a real holiday, not merely the one in her imagination.

But she responded, 'Yes, of course.'

'So come along, let's get over to the shop. I'd like to see you reunited with Dan's necklace.'

And as we walked across the street, I knew that Mrs Rutland's boundaries were far greater than the sum of those I had experienced.